For eight years now *Perry Rhodan* has been acknowledged to be the world's top-selling science fiction series. Originally published in magazine form in America, it has now appeared in hardback and paperback in the States.

Over five hundred *Perry Rhodan* clubs exist on the Continent and *Perry Rhodan* fan conventions are held annually. The first *Perry Rhodan* film, 'S.O.S. From Outer Space' has now also been released in Europe.

The series has sold over *seventy million* copies in Europe alone.

Also available in the *Perry Rhodan* series

ENTERPRISE STARDUST

K–H. Scheer and Walter Ernsting

Perry Rhodan 2

The Radiant Dome

Futura Publications Limited

A Futura Book

First published in Great Britain in 1974
by Futura Publications Limited
© Ace Publishing Corporation 1969

The series was created by Walter Ernsting and
Karl-Herbert Scheer, and translated and edited by
Wendayne Ackerman.

ISBN 0 8600 7009 3
Printed in Great Britain by
Hazell Watson & Viney Ltd
Aylesbury, Bucks

INTRODUCTION

PERRY RHODAN, commanding officer of the first manned terrestrial moon rocket, has returned to Earth. He has landed in the Gobi Desert, where he has established a base with the help of the supertechnology of the Arkonides, a human type race from the center of the galaxy whose explorer spaceship had crash-landed on the moon, where it was discovered by Perry Rhodan. Thanks to the equipment from the supertechnology of the Arkonides, the base in the Gobi Desert can defy any attack from the great powers of the Earth.

Perry Rhodan has already prevented World War III . . . but he wants much more! His goal is to bring about the unification of all mankind.

But mankind is not yet ready for Perry Rhodan's plans, and therefore, the battle continues for *The Radiant Dome.*

PART ONE

THE RADIANT DOME

CHAPTER ONE

". . . FOR THE TIME BEING I shall not even remotely consider giving up our position. I shall not resign myself to handing over to the NATO countries the knowledge acquired on our moon expedition."

The tall man with the lean face pushed down hard on the STOP button of his tape recorder. Both reels stopped abruptly.

Major Perry Rhodan, test pilot of the U.S. Space Force, commander of the first manned moon landing expedition, looked around in deep thought. The control panel center of the *Stardust* was as narrow and crowded as befitted a spaceship of her size.

The steel lids of both hatches, hermetically sealed during the space flight, were now wide-open. Through the thick quartz panes the vast yellow brown expanses of the Gobi Desert were visible. Only to the right of the moon rocket, which had landed here like an airplane, could some sparse vegetation be seen. This was the thin green strip growing on the banks of a small river known as Morin-gol. Just a few miles farther to the north, the river flowed in the big Goshun salt lake, whose southern shore formed part of the Chinese Mongolian border.

To the south of the *Stardust* lay the infamous central Gobi. Apart from a few small settlements nestled around the rare waterholes, and the military installations of the Asiatic Federation, there existed hardly a trace of human life in these desolate parts.

The grim realization flashed through Perry Rhodan's mind

that this desolation had been altered quite suddenly and radically.

Through narrowed eyes he gazed through the quartz window toward the east. Beyond the riverbed where the tiny settlement of Dashoba could barely be seen, quite a few things had changed. The military air base, formerly nothing but a miserable training camp, seemed to have turned overnight into a major airport.

The concentration of military forces was enormous. The massed troops of the outstanding Asiatic elite units evoked the impression that they were getting ready for an invasion.

Rhodan's eye wandered over to the tent close to the moon rocket. The comforting thought of absolute security became nothing but an illusion as soon as Rhodan examined it more closely. Once the tent had been part of the equipment of an Asiatic transport commando, which had arrived only one week earlier. Rhodan's lips widened into an amused smirk when he punched the START button of his recording machine.

When he began to speak again, his voice sounded somehow easier and more confident.

"I am making this tape recording to safeguard against any unforeseen eventualities. I repeat: This is Perry Rhodan speaking, commanding officer of the U.S. spaceship *Stardust*, test pilot working with the Space Exploration Department of Nevada Spaceport. It is extremely important to me to record our recent experiences with the utmost accuracy.

"Just one week ago Captain Reginald Bell returned from his daring special assignment. I could hardly believe my eyes, but he really accomplished the apparently impossible when he brought back with him the specialist for blood diseases who had so urgently been requested by our own ship's physician, Dr. Eric Manoli. The blood specialist is none other than the renowned Australian Dr. Frank M. Haggard, an outstanding research scientist, who gave the world the antileukemia serum. If there is anyone on this planet who might succeed in saving the life of the alien Arkonide, Khrest, whom we have brought back to Earth with us from our recent moon trip, Dr. Haggard is that person. Thanks to him we are now in possession of a portable lab equipped with all the special instruments needed for a thorough examination and an exact diagnosis. Together with the *Stardust*'s own medical facilities there now exists some well founded hope that we will be able to cure Khrest. We have two great physicians and medications of all kinds, in addition to the necessary expert knowledge. I am no longer so pessimistic as I was yesterday and during the past week. I am positive that the final outbreak of a totally destructive atomic war has been prevented, thanks to the inconceivably powerful means of the aliens. On the other side of our protective screen lies the debris of heavy atomic rockets. They did not explode! Thora, the beautiful woman commander of the gigantic spaceship, has intervened from her base on the moon. Since the nuclear weapons of all terrestrial powers are based on fission or fusion reactions, all that was necessary was for her to bind the free neutrons, rendering impossible any nuclear process that depends on neutrons. Our situation is not too bad; at least it is no worse than it was shortly after my desperate landing in the Gobi Desert. I firmly believe I have acted right toward humanity, as well as my own conscience, by refusing to surrender the technical scientific potential of an infinitely superior intelligent alien race to one single group of humans. Nothing, though, could ever shatter my belief in all mankind! Nothing will ever shake my conviction that the future of the human race must be based on a union of all those creatures who are known as Homo sapiens. It seems as if a time of trial has begun for all citizens of Terra. There is still a great deal of ignorance, mistrust, hatred and envy. The leaders who rule the various governments will be feverishly endeavoring to win for themselves and their countries' selfish interests the overpowering treasures of the Arkonides' knowledge. But this is definitely not compatible with a mutual improvement of the fate of the entire human population.

"If my grand plan is to have a chance of success, then Khrest's full recovery is an absolute necessity. I want to win him over to become the friend and teacher of the entire human race. Therefore, I fervently hope that Dr. Haggard will prove once more his expert medical knowledge and skill in healing our alien guest."

Rhodan turned off the tape recorder, quickly and somewhat abruptly, but not without good reason. He was not one of those men who are inclined to put down their thoughts and views in a more or less accomplished manner on tape, while being exposed to an intense bombardment by powerful weapons of all kinds.

His face, which had looked so relaxed just now, suddenly became drawn and intense. His hand slid to his holster quite instinctively, and at the same time he jumped to take cover. At once his cool, reasoning mind became aware of the absurdity of his unconscious reaction.

Rhodan stood up straight again while muttering an angry curse. What nonsense to attempt to find cover under such questionable circumstances. Either the defense screen of pure energy supplied by the Arkonides was working effectively or the massed military might of a gigantic army would shortly destroy them.

Rhodan swung his short weapon back over his shoulder. Leaving the rocket through the big air lock situated in the now completely emptied storeroom just behind their tiny cabin, he bounded down the ramp. At the same time a voice came over his intercom. In rather loud and unmelodious tones he heard a sarcastic statement:

"How dare you interrupt my well deserved sleep? Okay, are you still standing on your own two feet, or have they gotten you already?"

"Radio silence, please!" replied Rhodan, "I'll be right there."

He switched off his small wrist radio while speculating with a furrowed brow how far the Asiatic radio surveillance had succeeded in perfecting their efficiency.

The faraway thunder intensified to a mighty roar. Rhodan looked up toward the almost imperceptibly vibrating energy screen. The energy bell reached its highest point at almost 6,000 feet. This time, though, the enemy seemed to have decided to attack them in a different way.

Rhodan's mouth became a pencil thin line. His day old beard looked dark and rough on his tanned skin. A few hurried paces brought him to the entrance of the big tent.

Captain Reginald Bell no longer wore the uniform of the space force. It would have proved more than a hindrance on his daring trip to the "civilized" world.

"End of the world, late summer, seventh decade, twentieth century," he uttered in a throaty voice. "And I thought they had finally given up! Or have they found something in the meantime that will penetrate our protective screen?"

A silent threat was expressed in Rhodan's glance toward the enemy's distant positions. But soon he relaxed and silently offered a cigarette to his friend. A few soothing puffs later, he could even joke, "They mean so well, don't they? They have the best intentions. . . ."

His last words were drowned by the deafening explosions of detonating missiles. The normally invisible wall composed of lines of inconceivable energy began to light up in the blinding fire of exploding charges.

Rhodan started up again, "No more conventional artillery! If I am not completely mistaken, there must be some clever brains among the chiefs of staff of the Asiatic armies. They seem to have understood that normal guns are more than senseless within the range of an antigravity field. So what do smart men resort to, when they can no longer set up big cannons with their enormously strong recoil in such zero gravity conditions? They will use rocket missiles, of course! Or . . . ?"

Reginald Bell nodded in affirmation. A deep drag on his cigarette made it glow brightly. It was obvious that the *Stardust*, standing right in the center of the protective energy bell, had become the target of at least 1,000 rocket batteries. Judging by the hits, the Asiatics must be using at least 4,000 automatic rocket projectors of varying caliber.

The roar became unbearable. Reg had to scream to make himself understood. "But they have no atomic charges," he shouted into Rhodan's ear. "Thora has promised to intervene immediately. The antineutron screen extends over the whole Earth."

Rhodan was aware that Reg was yelling at the top of his lungs, but he could understand nothing of what Bell said. It was only a few moments until the hefty man with the massive shoulders realized the futility of his effort. Reg's mouth closed tight, and his broad face began to twitch.

The tremendous shockwaves released by the fast exploding projectiles were stopped by the energy screen. The men were safe inside, but the huge dome of pure energy seemed to vibrate like a resonance chamber.

High intensity barrage! registered Rhodan, glancing once again around the enemy's encircling battle positions. The soldiers of the Asiatic elite troops were entrenched in a wide ring that afforded them excellent cover. There were their rocket launchers and ammunition depots, all firmly imbedded in cement.

Nothing was visible, not even the smallest object, that had not been fastened tight to the ground with the greatest of care. Perry Rhodan knew that the soldiers were wearing special harnesses that anchored them securely to these stationary objects. The Asiatic High Command had brought in men who had been involved before in manned spaceflight. Others had gone through quick conditioning courses that prepared them for the effects of zero gravity.

Thus the element of surprises was lost. Although the marvelous defensive weapon of the Arkonides, the gravity neutralizer, was still as effective as before, it had, nevertheless, lost its practical importance.

Perry Rhodan realized that despite the far superior arms and equipment they had at their disposal thanks to the Arkonide supertechnology, they still must not underestimate the massed potential of an excellently trained army.

The constant barrage of heaviest rocket batteries could not fail to affect them inside the energy bell, even if the enemy did not succeed in penetrating the protective screen.

The nervous strain of unremitting innumerable detonations awakened the slumbering fear psychoses in their unconscious minds. And these fears, churned up to the surface of their awareness, threatened to shatter their inner powers of resistance.

Suddenly Dr. Eric Manoli, physician on board the *Stardust* and fellow conqueror of the moon, suddenly came charging through the tent's entrance and disappeared lightning fast through the moon rocket's opened air lock.

Rhodan needed but an instant to grasp the reason for the slender man's wild rushing about.

Instinctively both Rhodan and Reg began running. But Rhodan knew well that all their movements were observed by the enemy's optical position finders. Although the energy dome was impenetrable to material objects, it still let light-waves pass through, and everything within the invisible protective wall could be seen plainly from the outside. It could only aggravate their position if they were observed rushing madly toward the *Stardust* shortly after the onset of the bombardment.

For heaven's sake! thought Rhodan, alarmed, Don't let's display our vulnerable spots to them!

Rhodan and Reg met Dr. Manoli inside the big storage compartment of the ship. He was wearing the huge special ear protectors they had worn during the initial launching of their spaceship on their trip to the moon. How helpful they had proved in shutting out the noises of the blast-off!

Manoli was smiling. His lips were moving while his hand pointed toward the plugs of the connecting cables.

As soon as Rhodan slipped the heavy earphones over his head, the infernal roar dimmed to a distant murmur. Quickly he adjusted his throat mike and plugged it into the walkie-talkie on his chest.

"It was about time," Manoli's voice said calmly over the tiny speakers within the ear protectors. "I only wonder that it took them so long to get around to using such an intensive barrage. Seems that the gentlemen over there must have consulted some professors of the psychology department."

Dr. Manoli managed a faint smile, but his twitching lips belied his pretended composure.

"Thanks a lot for this splendid suggestion," replied Rhodan. "I should have thought of it right away myself."

"Why don't you let him get credit for something once in a while?" came Reg's voice. "How about a brainstorm on your part now?"

"The only message I am getting here is a feeling of miserable fear," retorted Rhodan dryly. "Fear caused by this energy screen, whose structure is unknown to me and whose potential and limitations are an unknown equation as far as I am concerned. But of one thing I am sure—they will try to wear down our forces of resistance by this uninterrupted heavy bombardment. Since their nuclear warheads have been rendered ineffective, they are now using simple chemical explosives. If that should not work, the next step will be harmless gases. Finally, if all else has failed, they might call in the experts on bacteriological warfare. There are quite a few possibilities that may not have occurred to our good Khrest. After all, man is a tremendously ingenious creature, and by becoming the Third Power and challenging them we have created a situation that has aroused and united all the scientific minds of the world."

"Sure, we have forced them to join forces," interjected Manoli. "Their super weapons have become useless. No longer are atomic reactions possible. Nothing can be done there without free neutrons, and Thora has eliminated those."

Rhodan cast a devastating glance at Reg, who turned pale. His tongue flicked across his lips. "What's the matter?" he inquired throatily. Ever since he had come back under Rhodan's immediate command, he had lost his boyish exuberance. His initial boundless joy over the overwhelming defensive weapons of the Arkonides had evaporated just as fast as it had generated during his trip to Australia.

Rhodan did not answer. He hurried over to the tent and handed the protecting earphones to Dr. Frank Haggard, the blood specialist from Down Under, who had just made his appearance, looking most distraught. The tall, heavy-set man understood at once. He vanished without a word into the interior of the huge inflatable structure made of tough artificial material.

They followed slowly. The first class soundproofing of the tent helped even further to deaden the enervating explosions of the bombardment. The threat of being worn down by noise was thus removed.

They walked past the brightly humming barrel shaped reactor, which had supplied the energy for the force ever since they had landed here. Once again Perry Rhodan tried to penetrate the shielding plates with his imagination in order to comprehend its function. Rhodan was a nuclear physicist and an astronaut. Although he grasped every detail of the nucleo-chemical engines of the *Stardust*, here he seemed to face an insurmountable wall. All his Earthly scientific schooling came to naught when faced with the alien's superior technology. All he knew was that the energies of a small sun were set free in the "Hot" part of the Arkonide reactor. This was probably based on an incredibly complicated process of fusion of the carbon cycle, which was as far removed from the fission reaction known and used by Earth's scientists as is Stone Age ax from a rocket machine gun.

Khrest had made the assertion that this apparatus, which stood no higher than six feet, was capable of supplying the entire industry of the world with electric current. Rhodan felt dizzy simply trying to figure out this immense potential. He gave up, as he had done before, trying to comprehend the superhuman achievements of the Arkonide race. For the time being he could do nothing but accept the fact that the reactor did work.

Heavy cables, as thick as a man's arm, led upward to the strange looking spherical antenna that radiated the huge dome of energy. The dome had a diameter of almost two and a half miles at its base and was a mile and a quarter high at its apex.

Six weeks had gone by since they had found the gigantic space sphere on the moon during the first manned lunar expedition. About six weeks should be entirely sufficient to let the great minds of Earth arrive at rather dangerous conclusions. By now they probably had seen through Rhodan's fairy tales about discovering the remains of an alien culture on the Earth's natural satellite. They were no fools! These men of the military and scientific commands of the mighty power blocs were smart thinkers. And if they all banded together in the face of common danger, the situation would begin to turn critical for the crew of the *Stardust* and its guests.

Perry Rhodan became aware of the questioning glances of his men, who kept observing him. Dr. Haggard's shadow was invisible on the curtain that divided the back part of the room. Quite obviously he had given a set of protective earphones to the alien who was resting there.

Rhodan's face assumed an impervious expression. For the past few days he had been walking about with hunched shoulders, which made his lean, tall body seem to shrink somehow. Reg was observing him with increasing alarm. Once their commander started losing his cool, everything threatened to go to pieces. Even he, Reginald Bell, was not the right man to lead to its proper conclusion the plan that had been initiated. He was far too impulsive for such a task.

Dr. Eric Manoli, physician on board the *Stardust*, would have been entirely unsuited to carrying on the daring enterprise. His qualifications were purely medical and scientific; he was completely lacking the ability to give uncompromising orders.

Captain Clark G. Fletcher had disappeared without a trace a week earlier. Rhodan was certain that Fletch, the fourth man of the *Stardust*'s original team, must have encountered great difficulties—and possibly foul play. It was even quite probable that he was no longer alive. How utterly wrong had been his decision to permit Fletch to return home! It simply could not end well!

Rhodan's mouth formed a firm thin line. Since he had not plugged his walkie-talkie in again, this was a hint for Reg not to question him any further. Instead, Reg's hand grasped, with an unconscious move, the silvery rod that he knew to conceal undreamed of powers.

It was the so-called psychoradiator of the Arkonides, a weapon that could block the conscious will of other people and force them to execute acts contrary to their own conviction.

This instrument was relatively harmless, though. It did not leave any damaging psychological aftereffects; neither did it put any undue strain on the target's mind. Unfortunately for Rhodan's men, the psychoradiator had already lost its initial element of surprise. The "other side" had recognized that the instrument's range was limited to about a mile and a quarter.

Thus the Third Power, as the *Stardust*'s crew had lately come to be known, had been forced into a defensive position.

Rhodan walked past Dr. Haggard's special mobile laboratory, which had arrived barely a week ago.

Reg shrugged his shoulders in answer to Rhodan's ironic glance. Reg was certain that he could not have brought the doctor through enemy territory under the present circumstances. But what did it matter now, as long as he *had* managed to bring Dr. Haggard here and, more important, perhaps, had brought along the means to cure Khrest?

Absentmindedly Perry Rhodan's right hand slid over to his

left shoulder. It should have encountered the military insignia of his handsome uniform of the U.S. Space Force. But in a flash he remembered that he himself had detached them. There was no longer a Major Rhodan, particularly since he had been officially deprived of his military rank via radio communication. Rhodan had become World Enemy Number One.

Carefully he drew aside the curtain. Dr. Manoli approached him. Quickly he plugged in the cables to establish communication between them.

"Don't worry any more than necessary," Dr. Manoli said calmly over the ear protectors' speakers. "He is feverish, of course. We were all prepared for this, that a biologically divergent alien being would not respond in the same manner to our medications as we would. His blood count is not unfavorable. The abnormal increase of his white blood cells went down soon after the first injection of Dr. Haggard's antileukemia serum. The disease has at least been arrested. The swelling of his glands and the subcutaneous bleeding are subsiding. But we can't explain the strange side effects. They never occur in human patients. But in the meantime we have learned a great deal about Khrest's organism.

"His metabolism is similar to ours. He also breathes oxygen, and his lungs let this life sustaining gas diffuse into his bloodstream. Both Dr. Haggard and myself," continued Dr. Manoli, "are agreed on this point. We administered the serum only after the most careful examinations. He will get his second injection within the hour."

"Despite the considerable side effects?"

"Despite them," nodded Dr. Manoli briefly. His face grew stern. "We can't avoid risks completely. Haggard is an outstanding specialist but not a magician. These side effects are well within our ability to control. Just pray that Khrest's organism does not suddenly collapse. Yet his circulatory system seems unusually stable. Perhaps this is due to the one organ in his body that we don't have, unfortunately. We have located a fabulously constructed pressure regulator above his heart. Our diagnostic instruments have analyzed it to become effective with the first signs of impending circulatory collapse by balancing and eliminating any constrictions of blood vessels or closing of capillaries. What a surprising body—hardly to be expected in a member of such a degenerated race. We are dealing here with supremely intelligent minds that are unable to make the necessary effort to transform their brilliant knowledge into practical deeds because they lack willpower. That seems to be at the root of their trouble, Commander Rhodan."

"Forget that bit about 'Commander'!"

"For me you will always remain the commander. The way it looks now, we have well founded hopes that Khrest will recover one hundred percent."

Rhodan looked at the incredibly young appearing face of the patient, whose forehead was bathed in fine pearls of sweat. Khrest was not a child of this planet; still he was capable of perspiring. A good sign, according to Dr. Manoli.

Rhodan turned away. The high intensity barrage kept on incessantly. Strong concussions caused the ground to shake. It was as if the enemy exploded their heaviest charges in the air just at the outer limits of the protective energy bell.

"I don't like it," whispered Reg. "They must be planning something. It almost seems as if these fire tricks are nothing but an attempt at diversion."

"If only we could ask Khrest if the energy screen will withstand these constant impacts indefinitely," said Rhodan. "Eric, could you rouse Khrest out of this semi-conscious state for just a few moments?"

"Absolutely impossible," said the physician. "This would be the greatest mistake we could make."

"You are quite right there," confirmed Rhodan. Then he began to smile softly.

Reg felt a shiver run down his spine. He was well acquainted with Rhodan's infamous gentleness, which usually ended suddenly in hard, ruthless action.

"If Khrest fails to recover, we are in for hell," stated the commander with apparent composure. "A hell worse than Hades, my dear friends! I have landed the *Stardust* here in the Gobi Desert against all orders. I have refused to surrender Khrest. I have kept emphasizing that none of the power groups of this world could obtain his superior scientific technological knowledge for its own purposes. We have suppressed an imminent atomic war, and we have made fun of the mighty armies with the help of the aliens' superior defensive weapons. They won't forget this so easily. The great power blocs of this planet have united against us. Up there on the moon, the alien woman commander of a gigantic space battleship is waiting for us to cure Khrest. These aliens left their distant worlds only for the purpose of searching for a planet, somewhere within the regions of our galactic position, that is supposed to possess the secret of biological cell regeneration. That would mean eternal life for Khrest. They want to preserve forever the brain of this genius.

"Thora, the female commanding officer, has also remained mentally active, like many of the women of her race. But she despises mankind because of our primitive level of development. Unless we succeed in restoring the health of this member of her race, we shall suddenly overnight confront the elite divisions of an outraged mankind, helpless and all alone. Then it will be curtains for our Third Power. Well, have I made myself clear?"

"Perfectly clear," replied Reginald Bell. "Crystal clear, my friend! In the event Thora withdraws, we will first pass through the cross-examinations of the Secret Service. This will be followed by an international court of justice."

"I can't see any criminal act in this, not even a mistake," said Dr. Manoli with calm emphasis. "It can never be wrong to act in the interest of all mankind. And this is exactly what we are doing. Haven't we accomplished a *rapprochment* overnight of the ideologically differing governments by a mere demonstration of our superior might. Is that nothing?"

"We managed to do that only thanks to *Thora's* superior power!" corrected Rhodan. "If Khrest should die, she will abandon us. Even if she can't start back to her home planet without our assistance, this will hardly disturb her. Fatalism is a characteristic of her race, after all. She will spin around herself a cocoon of an enormous field of energy, and she will reject as a matter of principle the idea of entering into relations with mankind. We have simply got to do something!"

"What?" The question came back sharply. Reg had reached that "certain point" of inner excitement.

"We ought to try to convince her that man is a tremendously ingenious creature," Rhodan said. "It won't be long until the enemy power possess nuclear weapons that can no longer be rendered harmless by an antineutron field."

Dr. Manoli turned pale.

Rhodan concluded without a trace of emotion, "Our secret research attempted to develop a 'cold' nuclear fusion process. If they should succeed, they no longer need worry about the antineutron field. Then I would not care to remain under this energy dome!" He squinted upward to where, far above the tent, the invisible energy screen formed a protective vaulted roof, against which the enemy's missiles were exploding like so many firecrackers. But that could change, and very quickly at that.

"Let's open our communication channel to Thora," said Rhodan with deliberation. "I urgently want to talk to her in my capacity as a representative of mankind who has to make a few demands in their favor."

"Demands," grinned Reg. "Did you say demands? She'll jump right out of the screen to scratch out my eyes. We are nothing but semi-intelligent monkeys, from her exalted point of view. According to her code she cannot get in touch with us or establish any mutually meaningful relationship. The affair with Khrest was a compromise she could barely tolerate."

Rhodan pulled over a small stool that had once been part of the equipment of an Asiatic transport commando. "If she has any drive for survival at all, she will listen and agree to my demands. Let's go; get the connection ready. You are our communications expert, after all."

Reg shrugged helplessly. Mumbling a curse under his breath, he disappeared behind the curtain. The peculiar videophone of the Arkonides had been set up near Khrest's couch. In any case, the roomy tent offered better accommodations for Khrest than did the tiny cabin of the *Stardust*.

"Do you intend to force her?" inquired Dr. Manoli worriedly.

"You guessed right," Rhodan replied slowly. "I have the impression that she is depending on Khrest far more than we imagine. I have noticed quite unmistakably that he is the one who gives the orders. I am no longer willing to play along with her with all that nonsense! Where will all this lead to if we have to beg her for help with every new incident? The moon is too far away for my taste under such circumstances. In case of emergency we shall lose decisive minutes and seconds. I need much more effective equipment here, with some offensive arms included. Please, no more questions now. If the things I suspect, way back in some secret corner of my mind, should happen, then Thora will snap to it. She underestimates the human race enormously. She simply can't believe we are capable of anything, which I consider a grave mistake on her part."

"I don't follow you," said Eric Manoli.

"You ought to think about it." Rhodan smiled sarcastically. "What do you do as a physician when a patient complains about some terrible pain? Do you give him constant morphine injections, or do you try to find the cause of his discomfort and treat the disease itself, rather than its symptoms?"

"Why, get to the root of the evil, of course."

"There you are," grinned Rhodan joylessly. "You got the point. The secret services of the great power blocs will also search for the root, which in this case is hidden on the moon. Or do you really think they still believe our fairy tales?"

Reg motioned to them. His bitter grimace could only mean that communication with the moon had been established.

Rhodan rose slowly and walked over to the curtained off partition. He stepped in front of the oval screen of the Arkonide videophone.

The aliens' vessel was on the far side of the Moon, the side normally out of sight from Earth. Contact therefore could never have been established by radio. When Khrest had been asked about this, he had only answered briefly that the faster than light radio technique of the Arkonides had long ago overcome such difficulties.

For an Earth engineer it was rather hard to accept such explanations. Mountains of further questions arose that, of course, were of more interest to the expert than to the layman.

On the screen appeared Thora's face—a three dimensional color picture of unique expressiveness. Thora was beautiful, breathtakingly beautiful, and yet of a startling impersonality in her self-imposed lack of warmth. Rhodan stared in fascination at her white blonde hair which formed a vivid contrast to her reddish golden eyes. Nevertheless, she was not an albino; this was just a characteristic of the Arkonide race.

Though Rhodan had been willing to address her just a moment ago with moderate words and to excuse her attitude by considering her upbringing, when he saw her expression he suddenly changed tactics.

"Just forget to explain to me that the time for our daily report has not yet come," he said sharply in place of a greeting. "Just listen closely and remember that I am no longer a pawn on your chessboard. If you are unable to remove the slight damages in the engines of your super spaceship in order to get it ready to start again, then you must consider yourself also incapable of impressing a human scientist and special soldier with your foolish behavior. The men of my race have more willpower and daring in their little fingers than your drowsy crew in all their decadent, hollow heads. And if your answer is simply to break off contact now, I shall switch off the energy screen at once. Did you want to say something?"

She stared at him speechlessly. Never before had anyone dared to speak to her, the commanding officer, in such a manner. But she did not break off communication.

Rhodan continued, "And now, will you pay close attention to what I have to say to you, madam! I . . ."

Reg became convinced that his former commander had gone crazy. He had assumed an attitude as if he were the chief of the powerful empire of the stars that Khrest once had referred to as the "Great Imperium." Rhodan seemed to overlook the fact that the planet Earth was nothing but a tiny speck within the Milky Way, just like a grain of sand in the Gobi Desert. Perhaps even less.

Reg was certain that this could come to no good end.

CHAPTER TWO

PARTNERSHIP and defense union mean neither more nor less than a genuine relationship of trust between the concerned parties.

When a worldwide union creates a special secret defense organization, the headquarters of such a group must be a a central position within easy reach of all concerned nations.

That is why the IIA, the International Intelligence Agency, had chosen the island of Greenland as a geographically favorable spot. The gigantic center of the NATO Defense had been built deep under the ground.

Allan D. Mercant was the all powerful chief of the IIA, responsible only to the Defense Union. The short, slender, unobtrusive looking man with the tanned, boyish face below a high domed forehead was a very peaceful person as far as the animal kingdom was concerned.

Allan D. Mercant could easily have passed for the president of the Society for the Prevention of Cruelty to Animals. He would have seemed in the right place if one could have observed him roaming the dense Canadian forests, his eyes shining and his camera poised to shoot.

Mercant was not at all in favor of hunting with a shotgun. This conflicted with his principles. His professional activities were therefore all the more astonishing. Malicious tongues had occasionally asserted that the well-being of one little animal mattered more to him than the life of any of his numerous secret agents. This was of course far removed from the truth, and Mercant was inclined to brush off such sarcastic remarks with a mild wave of his hand, while his eyes sparkled with amused irony.

At this exact moment, he was standing in front of a gigantic video screen. The light symbol in the upper right corner indicated that the TV camera was in faraway Asia.

This was certainly strange but would have seemed much more exciting less than a month ago. In any case, just now even the presence of Eastern officers and secret service men was no longer overwhelming.

Four weeks earlier it would have been unthinkable to permit access to the Greenland HQ of International Defense to any representative of the Asiatic Federation or even to one of the Eastern Bloc.

The crowning effect of all the incredible changes had been the personal invitations sent out by Mercant himself.

Thus it had happened that two Delta bombers of the Asiatic Federation and the Eastern Bloc had landed this very morning at the huge airport of the headquarters. The visitors had been welcomed by Allan D. Mercant in person. Nevertheless, this unpretentious looking man had been cautious enough to transport the strangers in a sealed train, which roared along one of the unfathomable underground tunnels deep down in Greenland's icy mainland. The strangers did not know exactly where they were. They were moving around now in a big, comfortably heated, well lit hall that gave no hint of being almost two miles below ice and rocky ground.

This was Mercant's center. This was the focal point of all lines of the Western Defense within the framework of a mighty defense union.

Volcanoes seemed to be roaring in the big, built-in concealed loudspeakers. The sound recording technique of the Chinese TV crews was excellent—perhaps too much so.

The viewing target was brought close by their excellent long focus lenses, and the eyes of the viewers were tortured by the constant bright lightning flashes across the screen.

The spectacle had already lasted for fifteen minutes. Conversation had become impossible among the men. They were watching in fascination. Suddenly Allan D. Mercant switched off the set, abruptly bringing back the attention of the spellbound observers.

Silence. Mercant moved his hand across his mirror-like bald head. He seemed so obviously harmless that Marshal Petronskij could not help but feel ill at ease and alarmed. The Chief of the Eastern Air and Space Defense looked helplessly over at the slim man with the expressionless face.

Iwan Martinowitsch Kosselow, Chief of the Secret Service of the Eastern Bloc, had not batted an eyelid during the TV demonstration. He seemed to think it was to his advantage to keep up his usual masklike face. Kosselow had fought many a battle in silence with Mercant, battles never known to the general public.

Two additional men seemed rather remarkable: Marshal Lao Lin-to, Commander in Chief of the Asiatic Federation Air and Space Forces, as well as the tall, raw-boned Southern Chinese Mao-tsen, who was known to be the Chief of the Asiatic Federation Secret Service.

Thus, the most important and influential personalities of the three major power groups of the world were assembled in the central bunker of HQ-IIA. It was amazing—really more than amazing.

The men looked at each other. The adjutants and minor experts remained quietly and discreetly in the background. This was the place where only the big bosses spoke.

Politely Mercant asked the gentlemen to enter the adjoining conference room. The last guards vanished. The room was hermetically sealed against the outside world.

Mercant's slight cough sounded like a revelation or perhaps, rather, a warning. Heads turned, fingers began to play with pens and pencils, wide awake brains became even more alert. What did Mercant want?

He spoke in the manner of a deeply caring physician whose psychological schooling has trained him to conceal the fact that he must operate. "I admire the tenacity of the Ochre army," he began charmingly.

"Gentlemen, despite all the efforts of the Asiatic Federation a brief study of the screen makes it quite clear that we are dealing here with a far superior opponent. The events of the past weeks prove, merely by the frightening collection of facts, that neither the NATO states nor those of the

East are involved here. I specifically want to have this point made clear. In addition I want you to confirm that you no longer regard the spaceship *Stardust* as a provoking base of the West within your own domain. These misunderstandings could easily have led to worldwide destruction in an atomic war. May I reassure you once more that the scientists of the Western powers do not have at their disposal any of the means and instruments that could produce such amazing effects and surprises. The *Stardust* has landed in the central Gobi Desert expressly against our will. Mister Mao-tsen, what is your opinion of this situation?"

The tall Chinese turned glumly toward him. Irony smoldered in his dark eyes. "What is that supposed to mean, Mercant?" rang out his deep voice. "I have come here to put an end to all these hide and seek games. I regret having to state that we have lost precious days and hours because of our mutual distrust. My sole concern is to find out how, when and where your Major Rhodan was able to lay his hands on these things. I have learned from a reliable source that these events are closely linked with the first landing on the moon."

"With the second landing, to be correct!" came an icy cold rejoinder.

Mercant's smiling face froze, as he recognized the unmistakable voice of the Chief of Eastern Defense. Marshal Petronskij managed a somber grin.

"I beg your pardon?" whispered Mercant.

"With the second landing of a manned spaceship," repeated Kosselow with studied impassiveness. "I have been authorized to inform you herewith. Our manned rocketship started three months before your *Stardust*. Since it is not our policy to publicize failures, the inexplicable crash of our spaceship was never made known to the world."

"May we have more details about this affair?" interjected General Pounder, Chief of the U.S. Space Explorations Command. His face was pale and perturbed as he turned toward Mercant. How could the Western Secret Service have remained in ignorance about such a vital bit of news?

"Gladly," Kosselow nodded obligingly. "What we need now is to make a clean sweep and to be absolutely truthful with each other. Our rocket crashed on the surface of the moon. Total loss, no news, no indications whatsoever. We have learned that your *Stardust* encountered similar difficulties, with the only difference that your crew managed to survive and even to return after their disastrous mission was completed. We have thoroughly examined the data you supplied us. We can therefore conclude that your rocket was thrown off-course shortly before trying to land by some disruption of its remote control steering system. This is exactly what happened to our vessel.

"This strange duplication of circumstances motivates us to ask for your cooperation. We are firmly convinced at this point that there is some mystery going on up there on our planet's satellite. It appears that your Major Rhodan countered this challenge more successfully than did our own people. At least, he was fortunate enough to survive this catastrophe. Whatever happened after their crash landing is beyond our comprehension. The only thing that matters here for us is this—both the Eastern and Western ships ran into dangerous complications as a result of spontaneous interferences with their remote control guidance systems. It is out of the question to hold any rival power groups responsible for this. These are the plain facts."

Allan D. Mercant nodded in affirmation. "Gentlemen, I have kept you fully informed of all explanations and information we have received from our Major Rhodan. Our former special test pilot stated flatly that on the moon he discovered the remains of a highly intelligent alien race from another system. This accounts also for the infinitely superior arms and instruments brought back on the *Stardust*. Despite our express orders the *Stardust* was brought down to Earth within the Gobi Desert. Ever since then he has refused any contact but has identified himself as the so-called Third Power. What he means by that is of secondary interest for the time being. But we are vitally interested in the plain facts that immediately confront us—especially the impenetrable energy screen that baffles our experts. We have just witnessed with our own eyes the senselessness of attacking it with conventional weapons."

"Let's get better ones!" hissed the Chinese bitterly. "Why don't you do something to straighten things out after the catastrophic treason of your special test pilot? We are all agreed that Perry Rhodan has become the world's greatest enemy. Unless we manage to remove the mysterious field of energy and to render harmless the men of the *Stardust* we—"

"Might even be forced by these circumstances to come to an agreement and cooperate with each other!" interrupted Mercant sarcastically.

Kosselow cleared his throat, then continued thoughtfully. "We are of the opinion that preventing an atomic war with the help of Rhodan's powerful weapons should not be looked upon as an ignominious deed," declared Marshal Petronskij. "Quite the contrary, gentlemen. It was you who pushed certain red buttons in wild panic. But your ballistic nuclear rocket did not explode, thanks to Rhodan and his secret defense arms. We owe it to Major Rhodan that we are assembled here today in a peaceful exchange of views. That is the other side of the coin. A very positive result out of a critical situation, and we should not forget it."

"No one is overlooking this aspect," remarked Mercant with professional seriousness. "On the other hand I'd like to remind you that the emergency buttons would never have been pushed if Rhodan had not landed on the territory of the Asiatic Federation. We have indicated in many communiques that this landing did not occur with our consent. Quite the contrary. Yet Peking has preferred to believe that we are involved in establishing a Western base in the central Gobi in order to provoke you. We ought to look at these problems in their proper persepective. All that matters now is to decide the manner in which this agreement should be reached."

"Something should be done," began Mao-tsen slowly. "We absolutely refuse to tolerate the presence of the so-called Third Power in the territories of the Asiatic Federation. Rhodan's actions are criminal according to our international laws. He is resisting and openly defying an internationally recognized government."

"Please, do consider Rhodan's point of view too," growled General Pounder. "I want to be frank with you. So permit me to state here that I consider it a distinct advantage for world peace if we are kept in check by a neutral power. Need I remind you how terribly tense and dangerous the political situation had grown? Rhodan's landing in the Gobi Desert was not the decisive factor in our pushing of panic buttons. Rhodan was probably nothing more than the spark that ignited the explosive tensions that had been building up for decades during the Cold War."

The Eastern Chief of Defense seemed to grow nervous. Dryly he replied, "General Pounder, you still appear to treat Rhodan like the spoiled problem child within the frame of your space travel program. May I point out to you that we, too, are unable to accept a new power that suddenly makes its entry into the constellation of the world's power groups. Quite apart from the legal situation, which has grown untenable by now, it is out of the question that we should be degraded to a position where we receive orders. Who can guarantee that Rhodan won't develop into a dictator ruling the whole world? Right now he is still small, practically immobilized, imprisoned by this mysterious protective shell. The time has come to employ the scientific and industrial might of all the great powers against Rhodan. First of all we should find out who is behind him. We doubt the validity of the information coming from the IIA!"

Allan D. Mercant rose, his face displaying displeasure. "I have asked you to come here to the headquarters of the IIA in order to familiarize you with the latest data available to my organization. All known facts were fed into the biggest and best computer brain on Earth. We were not concerned with determining whether it is advisable that humans be in possession of a superhuman technology. We wanted to know if Rhodan plans to play the role of a peaceful supervisor over mankind's future development or if he is inclined to turn into an imperialistic ruler with the help of infinitely superior instruments."

"The latter, of course!" Kosselow replied quickly. "What else could motivate him in his actions?"

"Please, be patient!" said Mercant with icy politeness. "As much as I personally welcome the opportunity of this meeting, on the other hand I detest the unlawful practices of a man who started out as a major in the space force and ends up returning to this globe as a dictator. So far it is still undecided whether Rhodan has done a favor for a nightmare haunted mankind.

"One thing, though, is certain—he has prevented a total atomic war. In this regard I must agree with General Pounder. All nuclear reactions have been rendered impossible. We have arrived at a temporary alliance, in which I can see the hopeful beginning signs of a future coalition between the great powers. All united, we are now confronting one man. These are the only important facts we need consider here. For weeks we have pondered the events that undoubtedly happened on the moon. You are familiar with Rhodan's allegations. You must have listened in to the radio communication between the U.S. Department of Space and Major Rhodan. According to that, Rhodan maintains his assertions that he has discovered on the moon the abandoned heritage of a far superior alien race. He claims to have appropriated these remains in the interests of all humanity. Therefore, he refuses to hand over these discoveries to any government of this world. This is tantamount to desertion and high treason. But cause and effect are not the same thing. Our usual standards of jurisdiction are no longer applicable in this case, particularly since Rhodan has renounced both his rank and his citizenship. He has no nationality, calls himself a citizen of the world and does not recognize the authority of our planet's courts of law."

"A legally untenable situation!" snapped Kosselow angrily.

"Indeed," confirmed Mercant. "Even more than that. The situation is utterly confusing. But let's wait with any decision until we can proceed effectively against Rhodan. For the time being we are limited to talk, which is not very productive in such circumstances. Let's rather get busy with the facts, for facts speak louder than words."

Mercant sat down. He motioned briefly with his left hand. A huge screen lit up, on which the launching of the manned moon rocket was projected.

The kinescope report of the ship could be seen, followed by the crew's preparations for the touchdown on the moon, filmed by the lunar expedition's own cameras. This was interspersed with the pictures taken by the manned satellite space station *Freedom I*. Rhodan's last radio message could be heard, then the shrill whistling of the automatic warning system and the high chirping of the call for help, "QQRXQ." The robot automatic steering system of the

Stardust registered the failure of the earthbound remote control steering signals. The last shots showed that the rocket was hurtling out of control toward the lunar surface. Finally the ship disappeared beyond the curvature of the moon.

Mercant indicated by raising his hand that the film projection was to be stopped.

"Gentlemen, you have just seen the preparations and the sudden plunge toward the moon's surface," he said. "So far everything was clear. We believed it an accident. Others spoke of sabotage. The only thing we are certain of is that the *Stardust* suddenly no longer responded to our remote control impulses, although her receivers were functioning perfectly, as has been proved by the return of the ship. These are the unassailable final results of our electronic computer. Will you listen now to the technicians' report of translated symbols of the final data. They prove without doubt that Perry Rhodan is not acting alone. We are dealing with an unknown and horrifying force. Therefore, it seems utterly senseless right now to present hair splitting arguments of who is right or wrong. What matters is solely in whose hands the power rests. If it is in Rhodan's, then we have no alternative but to remember with a resigned smile the old saying 'Might makes right.' Do you agree?"

Kosselow expressed his approval by a short resolute nod. But the representatives of the Asiatic Federation protested loudly.

Mercant shrugged his shoulders helplessly. "Mr. Mao-tsen, we are willing to accept your protests, but it is not in our power to undertake the necessary steps against Rhodan's invasion of your territory. You have tried it with your best elite troops and your latest arms. With what result, if I may ask? You are burning up millions of dollars by bombarding the indestructible wall of energy, without making as much as a dent in it. Rhodan does not even lift a finger. That means according to the laws of logic that he knows himself to be invulnerable. Give up, gentlemen, and be satisfied with hermetically sealing off this area. I will prove to you that the true danger is hidden up there on the moon. Rhodan plays nothing but a subordinate role here in this game with big stakes."

With these words Mercant had expressed in an indirect

manner what seemed to be the inevitable truth. He continued firmly, "In order to attack the evil at its roots we will be forced to go where the danger is, namely, to land on the moon and to attack it there. Listen first to this short report of our E brain."

Turning to the technicians, Mercant said, "Proceed!"

The loudspeakers began, "It is to be assumed that the data regarding start and emergency landing of the moon rocket are known. The return to Earth was executed with the assistance of electronic remote control system. Reentry into our atmosphere was accomplished successfully and according to plan. First indications of the preceding events lie in Major Rhodan's landing against orders in the central Gobi Desert. Our records of the *Stardust*'s construction and equipment show that the crew would have been absolutely incapable of using superior weapons and instruments before take-off. Yet after the touchdown in the Gobi Desert such installations were definitely aboard the *Stardust*. Therefore, it is concluded with utmost certainty that the commander of the *Stardust* must have discovered on the moon the nonterrestrial products of a nonterrestrial industry."

"Very clever!" muttered Mao-tsen caustically. "We already know that. Is that all?"

The monotonous sounds of the loudspeaker started up again, while the landing area with the moon rocket appeared on the screen.

"According to the confused statements of the test pilot Clark G. Fletcher, captain of the space force, we can conclude that the crew was forced by Major Rhodan to submit to the forbidden landing. Captain Fletcher was arrested and taken into custody by the Australian Security Service. Due to some careless procedures during a cross-examination, Captain Fletcher unfortunately suffered a fatal stroke. Judging by the tape recordings and medical records of the proceedings it appears that Captain Fletcher's memory bank was put out of commission by means of a parapsychic hypnotic bloc. Nevertheless, it is certain that at least Fletcher was made to obey his commander by force. The officials responsible for Fletcher's death are being prosecuted."

"How clever!" mumbled the Chinese with bitter sarcasm.

The report continued with a detailed account of the

various aspects of the investigation and its results. The attitude and behavior of the other two crew members, Dr. Eric Manoli and Captain Reginald Bell, were reconstructed. These were based on the sparse reports of far Eastern and Western secret service agents.

The statement was concluded with these words: "The mysterious disappearance of Dr. Frank Haggard, specialist for blood dyscrasia, must be looked upon as a significant coincidence. And evaluation of Rhodan's actions, while considering about 11 million probabilities, provides also the explanation for Dr. Haggard's continued absence. With a probability factor of ninety-nine percent it is stated that Major Rhodan must have brought back to Earth with him an alien being suffering from a serious blood disorder. An examination of all steps undertaken by Dr. Haggard immediately preceding his disappearance led to the inevitable conclusion that this disease must be leukemia. It is known which medications and special diagnostic instruments he has taken along. One hundred percent certainty!"

This time Mercant waited in vain for some biting remark of the Asiatic Federation Defense Chief. Mao-tsen sat rigidly in his chair, not uttering a sound.

"No, no, no!" breathed Kosselow heavily. That was the only sound in the room.

Mercant glanced at General Pounder, who seemed to be lost in deepest thought.

The report came to an end: "Rhodan's explanation of having found on the moon the ownerless heritage of a non-human race, and having appropriated and used these remains in a manner well-known by now, must be rejected as completely untrue! Careful checking of the scientific technical potential useful effects leads to the conclusion that it is entirely impossible for a human mind to comprehend the functioning of totally unknown machines and weapons within the span of a few days. The working mechanism of the so-called energy screen necessitates such specialized knowledge as is not at the disposal of our engineers. Even considering all facts, we calculate with one hundred percent certainty that even a highly qualified research team would have needed three to four years merely to understand the workings of the energy screen's mechanics. But another three to four years would have been required for them to learn how to master the correct procedures of working the apparatus. The intelligence quotients of our pilots are a matter of record. Even in intense collaboration they would never have been able to understand the instruments or to make them function. A careful calculation of sixty-four million possibilities results in the inescapable conclusion that Perry Rhodan, contrary to his statements, must have discovered on the moon alien creatures of surpassing intelligence. We cannot determine Rhodan's final goals, since we lack the necessary data. Therefore, it seems advisable to attack the base of the unknown aliens on the moon or, lacking suitable means of aggression, to try to enter into diplomatic relations with the strangers.".

With these words ended the report of the translated symbols of the mightiest E brain on Earth.

For the next two hours Mercant was kept busy answering the innumerable questions thrown at him by those present. Detailed calculations were requested and promptly supplied by the computer. The gigantic robot developed a crystal clear logic.

Finally Kosselow came to the heart of the matter. "We assume these final results to be correct. The E brain recommends that we attack the unknown danger on the moon by suitable means. But do you have such means at your disposal? Needless to mention here that our atomic weapons have been put out of commission. We can't even penetrate the screen around the *Stardust*. How about it, Mr. Mercant?"

The frail man looked around in a deliberate fashion. Then he inquired without his usual smile, "How far are you with your spaceships, Kosselow?"

"Our rocket has been ready to start for the past eight days. A crew of six men and a payload of ninety-two tons."

General Pounder let out his breath noisily. That was a new blow. Six men *and* ninety-two tons! The Eastern Bloc was still one step ahead.

"Marshal Lao Lin-to?"

"We are ready to launch our spaceship," declared the Commander in Chief of the Asiatic Federation Space Force, "with a crew of four men, payload of fifty-eight tons. The source of error leading to an explosion of our first moon-craft has been removed."

Mercant coughed dryly before he stated, "Our vessel will be ready to take off tomorrow too. The second manned Western moon rocket will be known as the *Stardust II*. The team will consist of four astronauts as before, with a payload of sixty-four tons. Please arrange for an immediate meeting of the parties concerned and their rocket experts. All these spaceships must leave Earth at the same moment, and calculations must be made to adjust for any differences in thrust, to enable the rockets to reach a certain orbit around the moon simultaneously. Will you be able to manage this?"

"What is all that nonsense supposed to accomplish?" interjected Kosselow roughly. "How and with what do you plan to attack? In case there really exists a base of alien intelligences up there our pilots will get the surprise of their lives. What do you intend to do?"

Mercant replied very softly, "First of all we must see to it that our ships will be guided manually. We will supply you with the appropriate radar equipment. The unknown base must be within a narrowly confined area on the far side of the lunar south pole. You will get shortly our exact coordinates. We know precisely where our ship started its emergency touchdown. The strangers have to be in that vicinity, a fact that was also confirmed by the calculations of the computer. We have been quite busy these last few days, obtaining a maximum amount of data. Are you willing to cooperate with the West?"

Another two hours passed before this problem was settled and put down in a written agreement spelling out the details of this special coalition. Afterward Mercant triumphantly played his last hand.

"You want to know how? Pay attention, please!"

This time an officer of the defense ministry switched on the video screen. A tiny island appeared on it, apparently uninhabited. The chaos started with an incandescent ball of gases. Unearthly rumblings emanated from the loudspeakers. A pillar of unchained primordial forces racing toward the clear blue sky. Tidal waves, horrendous heat, all hell let loose.

"The latest experiment of the Western scientists," declared Mercant matter of factly. "A 100 megaton fusion bomb. About three months ago we put into practice for the first time the theoretically known principle of 'cold' fission process. That means we no longer depend on an initial fission process. This 'catalyst bomb' uses only mesonic atoms. A chemically induced ignition of only 3,865 degrees Celsius is sufficient to begin the nuclear reaction. Free neutrons have thus become entirely superfluous. The new catalyst bomb will be ready for transport within two weeks and then become available for military use. Please advise your governments that each of your moon rockets will be equipped with one of these bombs. For the time being we do not want to employ this super bomb against Perry Rhodan's base in the Gobi Desert. If we destroy his cover on the moon, he will automatically have to surrender. Are there any more questions?"

Yes, indeed, there were still a number of questions, all pointing in the last analysis to one fact—never before had the great powers been as frank and sincere with each other as now.

A tall blond man with firm features and polite gestures kept close observation of the reactions of the almost almighty chief of the secret service. As soon as the meeting had come to an end, he requested to be relieved of his assignment as special observer and liaison officer with the International Intelligence Agency and to be sent instead to China.

Allan D. Mercant gave his consent. When the tall man left the room he could feel on the back of his neck the enigmatic glance of his boss. The rumor was that Allan D. Mercant possessed a brain with quite special properties. In any case he complied with the justified desire of his best special agent. If only he had not smiled so strangely! The heavy delta bombers of the guests roared along the runway; then HQ-IIA returned to its normal routine. Allan D. Mercant was satisfied, as far as such a feeling could arise within the framework of recent events.

However, he was supposed to have a parapsychic brain! And that fact had been overlooked by almost all the recent visitors to his headquarters. Only one man bore this in mind, and the thought became the source of everlasting disquietude for him.

"The dice are rolling now," whispered Mercant.

CHAPTER THREE

A FEW WEEKS LATER, at exactly two o'clock in the morning, the slenderly built officer with the rank insignia of a lieutenant general lowered his hand with a sudden jerking motion.

Almost instantaneously all hell broke loose. The mightiest guns and rocket batteries opened fire from 6,000 fiery mouths.

There had never been such a tremendous barrage in all the history of mankind's endless wars. At least, never had 1,500 batteries of mostly heavy caliber been directed against a single target about the size of a garden.

The blockade was still in effect. It had been augmented during the past four weeks by new divisions. The area within the energy screen had been cordoned off by five concentric rings of troops.

Some seconds after the opening of the sudden bombardment 6,000 guns of varying calibers continuously hit the protective bell. The target area was sixty feet above the ground and extended for 2,500 square yards.

Only there, nowhere else, were the exploding charges of the projectiles directed in a last attempt to pierce the wall of energy that had withstood all previous attacks.

The headquarters of the general in command were on a small hill, barely eight miles from the perimeter of Rhodan's domain. The gun emplacements lay farther to the north. The heaviest batteries had been positioned about eighteen miles behind the target area. Conventional guns had been put into action, after it had become obvious that the tiny forces of the enclosed enemy had become powerless.

Nothing could be noticed of the zero gravity conditions. Therefore, Lieutenant General Tai-tiang had ordered a new offensive.

His staff officers looked in fascination across to the target area of the energy screen. Among his staff there were several observers, in addition to the military experts. The force of impact of all the simultaneously exploding charges must amount to millions of tons. The spontaneously arising yet never ceasing waves of pressure would have sufficed to flatten a small mountain.

They kept up their observation for fifteen minutes without uttering a word. At this distance the target area looked like a white hot glowing spot the size of a palm from which constant flashes of lightning seemed to emanate.

The energy dome, which was invisible under normal circumstances, was aglow in a greenish shimmer that gradually changed to violet at the place of impact. Nothing else was to be seen. The radiant dome stood like a shining beacon in the reddish glow of the nocturnal sky.

"The strongest fortresses in the world would fall under this barrage," snarled Tai-tiang. "What kind of machines do they have over there? How can they resist this barrage so effortlessly, as if they dealt with glass marbles thrown against a steel wall? How do they manage this?"

The slender hipped Chinese turned his head abruptly. His eyes were burning. Tai-tiang was quite aware that he was about to let another billion of his precious national treasury go up in smoke by shooting at this mysterious obstacle.

"Our most venerable scientists hide themselves behind a perplexed silence," grumbled the general. "Very well! And your colleagues from the far West probably have no comment either."

American and European teams of observers had arrived fourteen days ago. The delegation of the Eastern Bloc had witnessed the catastrophe of the Asiatic army right from the beginning. Their freely given good advice had become less frequent. Now the Western advisors were regarded rather ironically.

A leading nuclear scientist from the United States tried to outshout the horrible roar of the distant guns. He barely managed to make himself understood.

"Sir, we have never pretended toward you or your government that we are in possession of miraculous powers or the philosopher's stone. We have encountered here an unscalable wall. Our scientific knowledge and the experiences of our technicians are failing us in the face of most mysterious forces. Therefore, I would suggest most urgently that you request again the help of the psychological and medical teams. If anything can be done here, then it must be accomplished by wearing down the surrounded enemy's nervous resistance."

"This is exactly what we are trying to do here," explained the commanding officer. "Why else would we have brought all these batteries here with such effort? We had to use the entire transport fleet of the Asiatic Federation Air Force to guarantee the necessary supply of ammunition. I simply can't understand why you can't come up with sensible calculations. Somehow it must be possible to destroy this structure! Even at the expense of another 1,500 batteries. We could find a way to secure them, just say the word!"

The discussions grew more and more violent, while a veritable inferno was unleashed just eight miles away.

"I would lose my mind over there," said a heavyset civilian. His eyes probed the tall figure in the semidarkness of the observation bunker.

The tall man stepped closer. His steps seemed to drag a little despite the unobtrusive elasticity of his gait. A narrow, restrained face became visible as he entered the weak cone of light coming from the dimmed lamps.

He did not speak. He lifted his field glasses to his eyes and peered toward the west. Then he glanced at his watch.

The bright flame of a cigarette lighter flickered in the darkness close to him. Lieutenant Peter Kosnow, special agent of the Eastern Secret Defense Service, was smoking nervously with quick puffs.

He was torn by violent emotions. It was not easy for him to stand here in this gathering of the highest ranking officers. Under normal circumstances Kosnow would not have given a damn about these military brass. His extraordinary powers of proxy had so far enabled him to get along well enough with them. Particularly since they had frequently been obliged to take orders from him, the low-ranking lieutenant of the secret service. This relationship had not been changed, at least not outwardly. As long as one could not read what went on behind Kosnow's forehead, he was still considered to be the representative of a powerful organization.

Yet he was convinced that any close observer must sense his inner unrest. As a result, he felt insecure and dissatisfied with himself. He was fighting to keep himself under control, while anxiously trying to avoid becoming suspect.

He ground out his half smoked cigarette. The bright glow died down. Only the narrow face of his companion was discernible in the reflected light from the video screen.

Kosnow began to feel doubts about his new won friend. He did not think for a moment that Captain Albrecht Klein, special agent of the International Intelligence Agency, would commit some stupidity. Even so, Kosnow regarded the daring of his blond colleague from "the other side" as sheer insanity.

Kosnow cleared his throat. The noisy argument between the officers and the scientists formed a welcome protective backdrop for their own discussion.

Albrecht Klein, who just three weeks ago had been personally advanced by Allan D. Mercant to the position of captain of the IIA, slowly let his field glasses sink. He observed the disputing men for a while; then an ironical smile played about his lips.

"What's the matter, friend? You look like a zombi."

Kosnow muttered a rough curse.

"The transport commando landed six hours ago in Siberia. By now your lovely moonship must have aboard it the Western power bomb. I don't like the whole thing."

Klein's mumbling stopped. He looked even more closely at the face of his Eastern comrade, who kept staring at the plainly visible energy dome.

"They are magnificent, aren't they?" he whispered into his friend's ear. "If only they had done the slightest wrong that could be considered an infraction of human rights, I would be both your and their most bitter enemy. But this way, I simply can't feel any animosity toward them. And this is what makes me sick. Can you understand that, my friend?"

Klein laughed shortly. "Who do you think you are talking to! Not only do I know that Rhodan has prevented an atomic war that had already started, but I also know that Rhodan has no intention whatsoever of favoring one of the parties. I am deadly afraid that things might change again tomorrow or the day after tomorrow. The terrible fear and mistrust of each other has disappeared from mankind, because a new opponent has arrived on the scene. They feel a common threat; therefore, they cooperate with each other. That is quite an accomplishment! We could not have wished for a better, faster and more peaceful way of attaining peace on this planet. As long as Rhodan exists as the Third Power we will be one united power. The longer he remains, the stronger will his incredible strength impress itself on mankind's awareness and the closer will our ties become. If only this state of affairs could reign for a few years or decades, then we would remain one united nation of this Earth. That's why I can't follow the argument that Rhodan must be destroyed at all costs. If he is defeated, the Cold War will start all over again. Let's be honest about it!"

"A clear and absolutely logical conclusion." Kosnow grinned joylessly. "There is only one flaw in your argument —we do not know in what direction Rhodan will develop as time goes on. He is only a human being, even if you are so completely enchanted by him."

"I am the only person to have spoken to him after his return to Earth. I am also the only human being, apart from Rhodan and his men, who has laid eyes on the alien Khrest. In the meantime our big bosses have also come to believe that there seems to be a nonhuman intelligence in Rhodan's party inside the energy bell. Quite remarkable powers of deduction, particularly since they have never seen Khrest. I am convinced that Rhodan is our man for the whole Earth. You ought to make a decision, Peter! Just think of the two of us! We are a living example of what the future might have in store for all men. But barely two months ago we reached instinctively for our weapons when we met for the first time."

"Routine. A conditioned reflex," corrected Kosnow.

"If you insist. But that is even worse if one has to look at it that way. Now I firmly believe it is our duty to do something for our fellow human beings. This latest rocket war, which was thwarted in the last moment by Rhodan's intervention, has given me the final push. Horrible when I think back how far things had gone already! We lived in constant fear of the next day. We must see to it that such a catastrophe cannot be repeated. One dud was more than enough for me. That's all I want to say on this point. Now to the immediate problem at hand.

"I have informed you about the outcome of the big conference in Greenland. The news about the catalyst bomb is kept a strict secret. No one here has any idea about it. Even Lieutenant General Tai-tiang is already too unimportant to be informed of this new kind of nuclear weapon. He simply carries out orders of the highest chiefs, who carefully planned this bombardment. As soon as the bombs fall on the moon, they will attack Rhodan here on his base. First the Chinese will evacuate the entire province; then a remote controlled Western bomber will appear and lay its egg. I don't like the way things are going."

Captain Klein glanced again at his watch. His dark coverall could hardly be distinguished against the unlit background of the bunker. Kosnow was silent. His strong teeth gnawed nervously at his lower lip. He was still hesitating.

"My mission will begin in eight minutes," Klein said. "You will be with me. Make up your mind by then. Here we can talk to each other without being disturbed."

Klein's tall figure disappeared in the darkness. A few seconds later he saluted several of the uniformed officers of the three secret services.

The representative of Asiatic Federation Defense was Major Butaan, the Eastern secret service's man was Colonel Kalingin and that of the IIA was Lieutenant Colonel Cretcher.

They had collaborated in preparing a mission to be carried out by a special commando of Eastern and Western special agents.

Peter Kosnow joined the group standing in the dim light. There was quick motioning, then a few loudly spoken words.

Lieutenant General Tai-tiang approached the waiting men. His salute was cordial, but his coal black eyes remained cold. "We will proceed as planned. Try to carry out the plan worked out by the defense services of our combined forces. If you should be successful you may rest assured of our gratitude. When will you enter the blockade zone?"

"At 3 o'clock sharp, sir," replied Captain Klein. "We want to request urgently that you will once gain inform the commanding officers of the concerned units about this exact time. We want to avoid being shot down by our own people by mistake."

The Chinese general briefly raised his eyebrows. Then he smiled. Apparently he had been startled momentarily by the term "our own people."

"You can rely on us. There will be no errors on our part. Your plane is waiting for you, gentlemen."

"It is getting late, sir," urged Lieutenant Colonel Cretcher. "Our people must return before daybreak."

"We should at least have established contact before sunrise," added Colonel Kalingin. "If Rhodan reacts according to our plans, you may cease fire by 8 o'clock."

"Let's hope so!" muttered Tai-tiang. "Be careful and see to it that you don't infect my own soldiers. What exactly are we dealing with here?"

"This is a discovery by Western research scientists, sir," answered Cretcher. "Would you excuse us please now!"

Klein and Kosnow followed the defense officers downstairs. One room of the bunker had been arranged as the center of command of the secret services. A physician gave the men an injection with a high pressure syringe that made the medication enter directly into their bloodstream.

"Do you feel anything?" asked the doctor after a few moments. "Dizziness, loss of balance or heat sensation?"

"Nothing whatsoever, Doctor," replied Klein. "Let's hope this stuff really works. I wouldn't want to swell up like a balloon or maybe shrink like a wrinkled apple and scare my fellow human beings after my return."

"You'd never get that far, if you should be infected,"

stated a radio bacteriologist with a horrifying matter of fact tone. "The artificially cultivated causative agents are perfectly viable and capable of reproducing under the local conditions. All you need to do is to open the valve of the pressurized cylinder very slightly. You will hear a certain hissing sound. Watch for it and remember that you must avoid squirting the plasma into your own faces—it wouldn't be advisable even if you are protected by this shot of antibodies. This culture is a highly concentrated solution of the most dangerous microbes. This is all I am permitted to tell you about it."

"Will this cause everything within the energy dome to become contaminated?" inquired Kosnow anxiously.

"What else did you think?" said Colonel Kalingin. "If you succeed in introducing this radio biological weapon inside the energy bell, all life will become extinct there within a few hours. Then our work here will be completed. Even Dr. Haggard does not know of any antidote against it."

Captain Klein's throat suddenly felt raw as he took the small steel bottle, no larger than a hand. It looked like a miniature oxygen cylinder. But instead of life sustaining oxygen it contained the most hellish brew ever devised in a secret laboratory of biological warfare.

Colonel Cretcher sensed his agent's reaction of utter disgust. He explained in a soothing manner, "Klein, you are being sent on this mission by the recognized representatives of all mankind. Perry Rhodan seems to place some confidence in you. Three weeks ago he permitted you to enter his energy screen fortress for a short interview. Try to get another one. Pretend to have slipped through the lines against the will of our chief of the troops, because you want to negotiate with Rhodan on behalf of a revolutionary resistance group. You have one important point in your favor —he knows you already. As soon as you are inside the energy dome, open the valves of the pressurized bottles unobtrusively. Even if you manage to release only one charge into the air, it should do the trick. Just think up a good excuse to make Rhodan believe in your mission. That's all."

Klein swallowed hard. His eyes burned in his pale face. "Yes, sir," he said with some effort. "Sir, I have carried out many an unpleasant order, but this one has them all beat. A really dirty job."

"A special agent's job has never been noted for its lack of ruthlessness," snorted Kalingin. "How dare you even raise such objections! We are not used to this kind of behavior from our own people."

Colonel Cretcher's face expressed disapproval, while Peter Kosnow stared ahead blankly.

"That's it!" hissed Major Butaan. This was all he said, but it was enough to make Klein understand that he had acquired a dangerous opponent in the Malayan.

The American radio biologist stated calmly, "Captain Klein, I fully appreciate your qualms of conscience. But rest assured, we did not bring here our most devilish weapons. These bacteria will cause swift infection and swelling of the tissues. But if one can administer the antidote within eight hours, there will be complete recovery. We are in possession of these remedies. It will be up to Perry Rhodan, therefore, to act according to our instructions, given over the radio and over the loudspeakers, and to leave the blockaded zone within these eight hours. This seems a rather humane procedure as far as I am concerned."

Klein did not reply. It would have made no sense to do so and could have endangered his position. The Asiatic Federation major was observing him with eyes full of distrust.

Before both men left, Butaan added with emphasis, "Our representative, Lieutenant Li Tschai-tung of the Asiatic Federation Secret Service, is waiting for you in the aircraft. It matters greatly to us to have him participate in a significant manner in this enterprise. Do we see eye to eye there, Captain Klein?"

The blond giant looked down on the slightly built Malaysian. "Why, of course, sir!" he countered politely. "I can't see any reason why Li Tschai-tung should not take part in our action."

Klein thought back to the ruthless manner in which his orders had been given to him. He had lived long enough in Asia to learn that commanders were not plagued by great sensitivity—especially in the Secret Service of the Asiatic Federation.

"In case of emergency you will have to sacrifice your own life!" he had been told. Klein could still feel the bitter taste in his mouth.

A few minutes later the men left. When they emerged from the underground bunker they were greeted by the infernal rumble of the guns. Farther to the north the sky, lit up by unceasing gun flashes, looked like a bloodred ribbon made of flaming gases.

Outside the bunker they found the helicopter waiting with its pilot Lieutenant Li Tschai-tung. He, too, had received his last protective injections. The plan was to fly to the energy bell and land at a safe distance from the target area. There they were supposed to establish radio communication with Perry Rhodan.

The mighty machinery of the defense services had thus finally been set in motion. Nothing had been overlooked in the planning; no one had made any mistake. Yet nobody had the slightest inkling how well the three men of the team got along. No one suspected that they shared the common interest of preserving peace for the world's population.

These were the three men that took off into the bullet ridden night sky—an American of German descent, a Russian and a Chinese.

As they approached their destination, Li Tschai-tung asked with a slight chuckle, "Is everything okay? I hope you realize that we are risking our skins."

Kosnow grinned simply in reply. Then he turned to Klein with a strange tone of voice. "Let's be frank with each other, brother! How did things go with your mighty boss? Why were you so perturbed by his peculiar smile when he gave you permission for this special task? Didn't the idea of smuggling the bacteria into Rhodan's base originate in your own mind?"

Klein nodded affirmatively. His face had turned pale. There was deep worry glowing in his eyes as he said slowly, "Allan D. Mercant is a fabulous man, but you never know what is going on in his mind. Even the best psychologists can't figure him out. His actions are unpredictable. There is a rumor that he might be a mutant with unusual mental powers . . ."

"Not so unusual in this day and age of the atomic bomb."

"Certainly. But Mercant is too old for his parents to have suffered damage to their genes. He was born before the first atom bomb. There must be other causes for his special gifts. Natural mutants have been known to occur throughout the ages."

"What has this to do with your uneasiness? He let you go, didn't he?"

"He surely did!" confirmed Klein. "He even provided the biological weapon. But I could not help feeling when I took my leave from him that he was, could, read my mind, that he had seen through to the deepest depths of my most innermost thoughts. He behaved like a father who is up to his little son's tricks but pretends ignorance. A queasy feeling, I must admit."

The men grew silent.

Kosnow stubbed out his cigarette. With clear, logical precision he presented his ideas. "There are two possibilities. In case he knew what you intended to do, then he does not object if you warn Rhodan. This would mean that Mercant approves of Rhodan's actions. Perhaps he realizes that this way Rhodan is guaranteeing worldwide peace. It would be surprising after all if a man of Mercant's caliber did not arrive at these conclusions. On the other hand, if he did not see through you, then you were simply imagining things. Turn to the left here, Lil! Signal our ground troops with a light flare; otherwise, they'll send a high explosive charge into our backside."

This was the beginning of a strange mission, where three men felt deep inside that their commanding officers were totally in the wrong.

Captain Klein toyed with the small pressurized bottle. Before the helicopter set down he said seriously, "Just think that we produced this stuff in order to contaminate you with it in case of war. Great, isn't it?"

"Don't melt your snowball," jeered Kosnow. "We have similar tricks up our sleeves. I, too, have come to believe that it is high time to get rid of this nonsense once and for all. Nevertheless, we will have to discuss sometime our ideological differences."

"Let sleeping dogs lie!"

"Okay. First things first. I'm very anxious to meet Perry Rhodan!"

CHAPTER FOUR

THEY HAD TAKEN refuge behind the thick padding of their ear protectors, as if the exclusion of excessively strong sound-waves could somehow provide a panacea against the attack-ers' superior firepower.

Groaning, with panic in their eyes, they had put on these helmets a few seconds after the onset of the renewed attack. Then they had plugged in their walkie-talkies.

Perry Rhodan was convinced that the situation had become untenable. Events seemed to take on the aspect of catastrophe.

In a sudden rage Reginald Bell had attempted to influence the encircling troops with his psychoradiator. It turned out to be ineffective, since even the nearest soldiers had dug in beyond the silvery rod's range.

The gravity neutralizer, too, had become useless. There was simply nothing left to degravitize.

One hour after the start of the barrage the vibrations of the ground became unbearable. The reactor of the Arkon-ides began to glow in a bluish light. At the same time the energy dome changed color.

Rhodan guessed that the violent ground concussions had impaired the workings of the apparatus. With narrowed eyes he observed the incredible fireworks toward the right. He had given up by now trying to comprehend cause and effect here. This was more than a human brain was capable of understanding. He dared not think how long the protective dome could withstand the intense bombardment. The mysteriously glowing dome might not be anything to be worried about. Perhaps it was only the result of the increased output of the reactor.

On the other hand, this bluish glittering might indicate the approach of the catastrophic end. Ever since all projectiles had begun hitting the energy wall at precisely the same point, a tremendous shift of forces had resulted. Rhodan wondered with growing alarm whether such excessive stresses had been foreseen and compensated for. The Chinese had met the dome's challenge in a clever way, there was no doubt about that!

An hour passed. The incessant bombardment had turned the energy screen into a vibrating bell. Had there not been the fabulous noise absorbing ear protectors aboard the *Stardust*, at least Dr. Manoli, the least stable of the team, would have gone insane. This was more than his constitution could bear.

Bell and Rhodan faced the situation with a grim smile. They knew that unless help from the outside intervened, they were faced with an imminent crisis.

Rhodan was convinced that the final breakdown of the protective screen was inevitable within a short time. He stood motionless in front of the barrel shaped reactor and observed the nerveracking light phenomena. He could not perceive the increasingly noisier workings of the machine, since they were drowned out by the infernal uproar created by the impact of the exploding missiles.

The pitiful fluorescent tubes of the tent had been shattered long since. The hard desert ground seemed to absorb the vibrations and transmit them immediately in earthquake strength shockwaves. As far as this effect of the intense barrage was concerned, there was not much protection afforded to the *Stardust*'s crew by the surrounding radiant dome.

In order to have at least some light within the tent they had fastened a few battery lamps to the highly elastic bracing supports. Especially the sick bay had been provided with excellent lighting. Khrest, the alien being from the far depths of the galaxy, seemed to be approaching a crisis.

At the beginning of the heavy shelling Dr. Haggard had been startled out of his drugged sleep. Until then Dr. Manoli had watched over the patient.

Khrest's incredible circulatory system had apparently successfully overcome the strain of the second injection. Lab tests proved clearly that all symptoms of leukemia had disappeared. The hematology report was negative. Yet the stranger remained unconscious.

Cautiously Rhodan retreated from the reactor as if he feared that any moment might bring a holocaust from the suddenly bursting apparatus, whose workings mystified him.

Reginald Bell sat in front of the videoscreen of the *Stardust's* radar equipment. They had removed it from the moon rocket and taken care to install it to withstand vibrations as much as possible.

This radar equipment was of a highly specialized nature, particularly well constructed to function despite the greatest acceleration and the mightiest jolts. The crash landing on the moon had failed to knock it out of commission, and the present heavy barrage did not seem to affect it.

On the radar screen could be seen with high magnification the positions of the enemy.

The infrared position finder showed excellent three-dimensional pictures of the gun embankments on the other side of the river. The automatic warning system functioned perfectly; still the attached robot brain could not manage to calculate the fluctuating position of the enemy.

No human being was visible within the six mile zone around the energy screen; no sign of life, no activity whatsoever that could have been pinpointed by the position finder or attacked with the help of the Arkonide arms.

Perry Rhodan, still wearing the uniform of the space force, hesitantly stepped closer. Once again his eyes fastened on the shining fluorescent screen. Bell's broad face was half-hidden under the enormous protective earpads. Only his eyes, clear as water, peeped out from close to the edge of the thick bulge. The throat mike around his neck had once again become the exclusive means of communication for the friends.

Rhodan established the contact with imperceptibly trembling hands. Right away he could hear the fast breathing of Bell.

"Only a few more hours and the reactor will be finished," he said quietly. "Are you aware of that?"

Bell turned his head. "And . . . ?"

Rhodan's lips formed a thin line. With a significant glance he looked at his watch. "We shouldn't expect miracles even from the products of a far superior technology. Clear thinking people with coolly reasoning brains can figure out that any mechanism might eventually fail." He laughed briefly in resignation, "that's exactly what is going to happen here. Unless there is still something else!"

Bell searched along the western perimeter of the encircling enemy positions. The delicate infrared radar equipment let them see even the glowing cigarettes of the Asiatic soldiers. On the screen a three-dimensional ring of widely dispersed flickering dots became visible. It was strange.

Bell did not fail to register Rhodan's short laugh correctly. Bell's pale face lost even more of its color, while his eyes were questioning.

"Unless there is still something else," repeated the commander, lost in thoughts. "They'll keep up this bombardment for hours. They are hoping for a collapse of our energy screen, but they are certain that our nerves won't hold out much longer. The only person who could understand the functioning of the reactor and who could regulate it again is Khrest. But he is deeply unconscious. This state might continue without endangering his health, but it certainly endangers all our lives! It will probably cost our lives! In case the reactor quits, whether it dies down quietly or explodes violently, we are lost. We are close to capitulating, do you understand?"

Bell kept staring at his radar screen. A new shockwave from the desert ground made the hanging lamps sway wildly. The shadows on the walls of the tent assumed horrifying distorted shapes. Beyond the partition both physicians seemed to jerk violently under the impact.

Bell looked up briefly from his screen and glanced toward the sickbay. Khrest's shadow was etched sharply on the dividing wall. Still motionless, he was resting on his couch. Several of the medical robot instruments of the Arkonides had been rendered unserviceable. They had obviously not been designed for extreme conditions. Now the physicians were forced to carry out the intermittent examinations of blood pressure, heartbeat and respiration personally. This was a demanding job, made especially difficult while dealing with an unknown organism.

"Yes, I do understand," Bell answered. "Khrest must wake up. I see no other way out." He grinned with a sly grimace. "Or call Thora. Your latest appeal to reason had no effect on her, though! Maybe it will finally sink in that things are getting serious here."

"The same thought has occurred to me, too," Rhodan replied slowly. His hand grasped the plug, and a fixed smile played around his lips.

"There is something still the matter, my friend! That fabulous Arkonide sender gave out just a couple of minutes ago. We are cut off. Would you like to try to repair it?"

Reginald Bell froze. The pallor of his face revealed all—he realized that their wonderful experiment was just about to fail miserably. But he caught himself quickly. Without a trace of panic he remarked, "That was to be expected. They unload tens of thousands of tons of explosives on our energy bell. In all likelihood they are also trying to detonate subterranean charges outside our area. They must intend to drive us insane with these artificially induced earthquakes. Okay, the set no longer functions. When will Thora notice it?"

"At her next daily communication. It's due at 8 A.M. If we fail to reply to her call, she will act."

Bell swallowed hard and painfully. The lean face of his former commanding officer had changed into a rigid mask.

"What do you mean by that?" inquired Bell hastily.

"What?" Rhodan turned the volume down on his loudspeaker. Bell's strong voice had blasted painfully against his eardrums.

"Despite the fact that we were upgraded by the scientist Khrest to class D of the intelligent galactic life forms, she still refuses to deal with us on an equal basis. In case we don't reply to her routine check, and as soon as her robot direction finders ascertain that our energy bell is under constant bombardment, she might assume that something has happened to all of us, particularly to Khrest. Then she will abandon all restraint and act exclusively as the commander of a space battleship. She had already been very close to teaching a most painful lesson to mankind. Okay, we'll soon know. How about it—do you want to tackle that repair job of the Arkonide sender?"

Rhodan's hand touched the plug of his walkie-talkie. His gray eyes were alight with a cold gleam. Bell could not help feel that Rhodan was just about to make a decision.

"I'd rather sit down on a red hot stove without the benefit of asbestos trousers." He squeezed out the words with determination. "What in hell do I understand about that thing! I couldn't even repair the smallest loose connection. I can't even open the metal casing. Our cutting tools won't even make a dent in it. I've tried everything I could think of. But this set has neither screws, clamps nor terminals. It looks as if it were cast out of one solid piece. Of course, it must be possible to get inside that mechanism somehow. Only don't expect me to do it. I just don't know how."

"You are absolutely certain of that?"

Bell simply nodded his head resolutely.

Rhodan stated with deliberate slowness, "You realize, don't you, that I shall never expose the human race to the wrath of a woman spaceship commander?"

Bell did not reply. He knew the answer.

"Well, then we are agreed on that."

"You ought to try to search for some way of informing her," Bell blurted out, quite alarmed. "If we surrender, then we should at least see to it that Khrest will first be rescued by her."

"That's exactly what I plan to do," declared Rhodan briefly. "If Khrest has not regained consciousness by 8 A.M. I shall get in touch with her via the main U.S. broadcast station at Nevada Fields. Our own sender is too weak to get through to her. If Allan D. Mercant is smart he will cooperate at once. He should realize that neither he nor others can claim Khrest for themselves. Thora can set free the Arkonide scientist Khrest at any moment she chooses. I'd rather not imagine what our fate would be afterward."

"Please, try it," whispered Bell with agitation. "For God's

sake, will you try it! There is no telling what she might do otherwise."

Rhodan switched off. Bell's desperate voice ceased abruptly.

Shortly after 3 A.M. Rhodan cautiously pushed aside the room divider curtains.

He saw Khrest's lean face, his high domed forehead bathed in perspiration. He was stretched out motionless on his couch.

Dr. Haggard turned around.

Rhodan quickly established contact via his walkie-talkie. "How is our patient, Doctor? Please, be frank with me. We have come to the end. The reactor has begun to change color in an ominous way. Our radio communication has been interrupted. How is he?"

Haggard obviously belonged to that race of men who do not know the meaning of the word "nervousness." He did not display the slightest excitement. "Some mysterious side effects could have been predicted," he declared calmly. "Khrest reacted favorably to the injections. The serum has done its work; his leukemia has been cured. His circulatory system is absolutely stable, and his heartbeat and pulse rate are normal. His blood count shows no abnormalities of any kind. But I have no idea why he is not coming to."

"He must regain consciousness, he simply must!" urged Rhodan. "By 8 o'clock he must be sufficiently awake to give us some vitally needed information. Unless I answer Thora's daily call, we are in for a major catastrophe."

"Why doesn't she come here with one of her auxiliary vessels?" the physician demanded angrily. "It should be child's play for her to help us in this desperate situation. I find her attitude rather incomprehensible. She entrusts to your care this dangerously ill man and permits him to be taken back to Earth with you. Yet she refuses to do the least thing to help his recovery. That is sheer insanity. If she is so anxious for him to get well again, you'd think she would do everything in her power to make sure of it."

"You fail to recognize the mentality of these people, Doctor," countered Rhodan. His face grew dark. "Thora is under the influence of a strong code of honor and racial prejudice. Her conditioning cannot be reversed within a few short weeks. In her opinion we are a very backward race. She neither desires nor is she permitted to take up relations with us. But if she ever does so, it may come in the form of a very painful lesson that might turn into horrible punishment if mankind ever dared to offend her exaggerated self-image as a member of the ruling galactic nation. Please try to understand her attitude from a purely psychological point of view."

"She ought to replace her education and arrogance with some logic," insisted Haggard. "If I found myself in a critical situation I would grasp at any straw."

"This is exactly what she did, when she entrusted Khrest to our care. She has foiled an atomic war and has created a volcano in the Sahara desert. The only reason for these actions was to ensure a safe stay on Earth for Khrest."

"Then she did not intervene out of concern for humanity's survival?"

"Not exclusively. We should not expect any miracles or heroic and benevolent deeds from her. Whatever we receive from the Arkonides in the form of knowledge and material goods will have to be paid for eventually. Thora has already committed acts that conflict with her own convictions. She has placed her confidence in us and done something forbidden by her honor code. Of course, she acted in an emergency. Her spaceship is unable to start. Her degenerate crew is incapable of repairing the damage. They simply neglected to take along any spare parts because of criminal frivolity. This race is at the end of its existence. Khrest, the last outstanding mind, is severely ill. Should he die or be harmed by any human being, Thora will regard our world and its inhabitants as sublevel forms of intelligent life. In her cold rage mostly fostered by her terribly offended self-confidence, she will start thinking about this human species. She will look upon us in the manner of a scientist who contemplates the fate of a beautiful but expendable guinea pig. She will deliberate on our future in a cold, logical, essentially prejudiced manner, which from our point of view appears to be unjust. I will not let it get to that point, Doctor! I have started this enterprise motivated by the desire to unite mankind in order to see it grow strong and happy. I shall not risk humanity's survival by insulting a representative of a superpowerful alien race. Did I make myself clear, Dr. Haggard?"

Rhodan's eyes seemed to consist of broken pieces of ice. Suddenly Haggard became aware of the suggestive power radiating from the icy stare of this tall, lean man.

He nodded feebly, his hands grasping his mike tightly. "What are your plans, Major?"

"Don't call me that. I have been stripped of my rank and dishonorably expelled from the space force. I shall try to save whatever is salvageable. If Khrest is not conscious by 8 o'clock, to help us reestablish radio communication, then I shall surrender. At least I know that lever that switches off the Arkonide reactor. That's at least something, isn't it!"

He let out a bitter laugh. Haggard looked at him thoughtfully. Rhodan continued with emphasis, "Doctor Haggard, Thora has excellent televisors. If the radio communication will not work, then she will have us at once under visual observation with these superior instruments. If the intense barrage should still continue, she would consider us to be in danger, or perhaps even dead. Then the world would experience the most horrible fate. I shall see to it that the bombardment ceases at 8 o'clock sharp. That is our last chance to forestall any rash acts by this impulsive woman. Only in the greatest of emergencies will she send a rescue craft down to our planet. By setting up this situation, I still risk that she will make some mistake, despite the cease fire.

"My plan is a compromise solution. It would be infinitely preferable if you could rouse Khrest before 8 o'clock. Our sender can be only slightly damaged. He will manage to reestablish contact with Thora. Try all that is humanly possible, Doctor. My second alternative is sheer desperation. I am convinced that the Chinese will abruptly stop the bombardment after my radio appeal to them. But can we be as sure of Thora's reactions?"

Rhodan shrugged his shoulders. Haggard averted his glance. He could not bear to look into Rhodan's strangely glittering eyes.

"What do you want me to do?" stammered the physician.

"Not much. Since you diagnosed Khrest's circulatory system as unusually stable, just inject some stimulating drugs.

You brought them along for such an eventuality, didn't you? Wake him up!"

Haggard hesitated. "I might risk everything this way. Do you realize that?"

"You won't risk any more than you already have. If he could withstand the antileukemia serum, then his organism will also manage to deal with stimulants. Activate his body. It must be possible to awaken him from this deep leaden sleep."

"I'll give him a shot of the same strength that can be tolerated by the average human being without harm," stated Dr. Haggard resolutely. "But not any stronger, not even a microgram more!"

"That will do fine," consented Rhodan. Suddenly his face became distorted. His hand whipped down to his holster and jerked out his gun while he spun his body with lightning speed.

All ready for action, he stopped dead in his tracks, staring at a can of beans that had hit him hard between his shoulder blades. Up front, hardly visible in the feeble glow of the radar screens, stood Bell, waving and shouting excitedly.

Rhodan vaulted over Khrest's couch. A few wide jumps brought him close to Bell. The plugs slid into place as if by themselves. The wild roar of the engineer became painfully audible in Rhodan's earphones.

"You seem to have protective padding on your back, too!" shouted the heavyset man. "That was the third can, my friend." His index finger stabbed wildly toward the radar screen. "Three small bodies, close to the ground, at a speed of eighteen to twenty miles per hour. Probably three people. Now they're clearly visible. I am going out of my mind. There are really three men with rotor flying engines!"

There was no doubt any longer. These were three persons, flying just above ground level, tiny rotor blades attached to their backs. They flew in precise formation straight toward the protective energy screen.

Reg started up again, "Looks as if they want to run head on into the energy wall. Odd, isn't it?" His excitement had given way to utter amazement.

Rhodan had walked over to the Arkonide reactor. Pushing

a small lever sufficed, as Khrest had explained some weeks ago, to change the structure of the energy screen, so as to render it permeable for ultrashort radio waves. It had previously permitted passage of Rhodan's own broadcasts, which presented an insoluble mystery for the trained mind of a human engineer. He could not explain it, though he had witnessed it with his own eyes.

Rhodan jumped back to the instruments. The big receiver of the *Stardust* was working now. A red bulb began to glow. The acoustical whistling signal was inaudible. The roaring detonations drowned out everything pitilessly.

They switched their portable F speakers over to the powerful receiver. A soft whisper came over the earphones: "Captain Albrecht Klein calling Major Perry Rhodan. Don't shoot! I am coming with two colleagues. You have met me before as Lieutenant Klein, from International Defense. I am broadcasting with minimal strength. Please come to the border of your enclosure. I must talk to you. We are waiting. Don't shoot. No danger."

Rhodan adjusted his instrument so that only Bell remained in contact with him. Without waiting for Rhodan's comment, Bell stated blandly, "Klein? Must have been promoted. Isn't that the guy that you let through the screen so carelessly? He saw Khrest then, didn't he? I don't like him."

"But I do. I'll take one of the trucks. You watch from here. When you hear from me the password 'Armageddon,' open the screen for exactly three seconds right in front of where I am standing, for just about an area of six by nine feet. I have already prepared for the structural change."

"You're crazy! If they use that moment to chase a remote controlled rocket right through the gap, that would mean curtains for all of us. Klein might carry such a gadget hidden on his body. I know these tricks, my dear friend. After all, I remember my days with the intelligence service. I will not open."

His gaze was clear, his eyes hard. But after having looked at Rhodan's masklike face for a few moments, he lowered his head. "Okay. Password 'Armageddon,' I'll wait for your signal."

Rhodan left, his heavy machine pistol, with the most dangerous microrack missiles, swinging over his shoulder. But far more dangerous was the silvery rod in his hand. The Arkonide psychoradiator was surprisingly effective at short range.

Rhodan was not willing to run any risks.

While outside, the gas turbine of the Chinese truck began running, Captain Reginald Bell stood still rooted to the ground, staring at the spot where Rhodan had just been. He still could feel the bright flicker in his commander's steely eyes.

Bell had been absolutely convinced he would foil Rhodan's project. Then he had nodded in agreement, without hesitation. He turned to his instrument panel. He was still pale and shaking. He firmly closed his eyelids, as if to shut out some picture.

The imaginary vision remained. Rhodan's burning glance seemed to have etched itself on his retina. Abruptly he opened his eyes.

Reginald Bell was a man with a strong character who could be a daredevil with well defined ambitions. He was a special pilot not giving to feelings of anxiety. But now he was experiencing fear.

He muttered a curse, then started to observe Rhodan, who was racing over the stone strewn desert landscape. Only a few sparse plants could grow there, since the area was too remote from the river with its life giving water.

Rhodan drove straight toward the point where the three bodies had touched ground. Bell kept him on course with several short corrections via walkie-talkie. He did so with a monotonous voice while his emotions were raging inside. How was it possible for Rhodan to have caused him to change his mind so quickly? How . . . ?

He was still pondering that question, when Rhodan suddenly stopped his car. He was close to the energy wall, and the time was 3:22 A.M.

The psychoradiator jerked upward in Rhodan's firm hand. Far over to the other's side there were the blinding fireworks of innumerable explosions, almost as bright as day. Only the three bodies in their dark overalls were discernible. They cowered close to the ground.

Rhodan's hand jerked upward. This signaled, "Get up," to the men on the other side of the energy wall.

CHAPTER FIVE

"ARMAGEDDON!" Bell received Rhodan's command over their two way radio and quickly carried out the manipulations to alter the structure of the energy wall according to Rhodan's instructions. Three bodies started to move with lightning speed.

Captain Albrecht Klein had never before run so fast. A few giant leaps brought him through the gap within the weakly glowing energy dome.

Against the background of the fiery thunderstorm of the incessant missile barrage Rhodan's tall figure had appeared so incredibly threatening, enigmatic and radiating an almost mystical influence, that Peter Kosnow instinctively grasped his hand weapon.

The silvery rod's bright glimmer had instantaneously rendered Kosnow incapable of action. He could still hear ringing in his ears the command that he had to obey unconditionally, even against his will.

"Stay where you are; don't move, don't act."

That had been all. Perry Rhodan had changed considerably. He was not the same man as a few short weeks ago when he had landed on Earth. Deep lines of worry and pain furrowed his face. His twitching lips indicated clearly that he seemed to have come to the end of the rope. His nervous resistance was giving out.

Klein looked around, stunned by the inferno of noise and vibration. He could never have imagined what the effect of the furious torrent of gunfire would be.

The Chinese defense officer, Li Tschai-tung, too, had been robbed of his willpower. The Arkonide psychoradiator had lost none of its effectiveness.

Albrecht Klein alone remained unaffected. He was in full possession of his conscious will and reasoning faculties. Instead he saw himself confronted by the threatening barrel of an automatic weapon, one of the new type Rak guns.

Cautiously Klein had raised his arms above his head, an unreal gesture inside the raging hell around him. Seconds later he realized that any discussion he had planned to have with Rhodan would have to wait until later. It was out of the question even to hear oneself think under these circumstances.

Klein then drove the car. Once inside the tent, he received from Rhodan a helmet connected to the intercommunication system. Then he could begin giving out some news.

Outside the energy dome the missiles kept up the steady rain of fire. Inside Lieutenant General Li Tai-tiang's commando bunker, many eyes attempted in vain to follow the events in the radiant dome.

Three high ranking secret service officers were calculating the odds that their agents would successfully complete their mission. If they managed to spray the contents of even one of the pressurized bottles, the downfall of the Third Power would be guaranteed.

Within the tent Captain Klein absorbed everything attentively. He missed neither the dangerously glowing reactor nor the fleeting shadows of the two physicians scurrying behind the dividing curtain.

Then he became aware of Rhodan's gaze on him, which he returned uneasily. He swallowed hard and audibly before he managed to say, "Many thanks, sir. Before we go any further, will you be so kind and examine the contents of the inside pockets of our overalls. You will find there on every one of us a steel bottle the size of a hand and as thick as a salami. We have been officially ordered to release their liquid contents once we got inside your compound."

Bell whirled around, his broad face contorted, his index finger playing with his Rak gun's trigger.

Rhodan remained in his rigid posture. Only his eyes had changed. They seemed to dissect Klein.

"Inside our breast pockets," urged Klein. "Won't you check, please? We have no time to lose. If our chiefs should have the slightest inkling we are standing here so peacefully in front of you, we need not even bother to return."

Rhodan remained silent, but Bell began to act. Neither Kosnow nor Li put up any resistance as the dangerous containers changed hands. Klein stared quietly at the small cylinders. He was startled by Rhodan's deep voice.

"Okay, Klein. That was that. What is inside these bottles?"

"A radio bacteriological weapon that would have finished all of you off within a few hours. This was my idea."

Klein was amazed at Rhodan's continued calm. Perry was now lowering his automatic gun.

"Your idea?" Bell asked coldly. "And now you want to play the big hero! What are you really up to? By the way, Klein, I would not have admitted you to our dome."

"That's a matter of opinion," interjected Rhodan dryly. "Captain, did you develop this plan with the bacteriological warfare because this would enable you to get in touch with me without arousing suspicion? I might possibly have hatched out a similar strategy myself, in your position."

Klein's respect grew tremendously. The strangeness of the situation seemed to become even more unreal, as he took in the alien instruments and gadgets inside the tent. Klein was glad that Kosnow's rather impulsive mind had temporarily been put out of action.

"You guessed right, sir. We even received orders to come up with some fictitious data to make you believe in some nonexistent resistance group. But more about that later. In any case you must realize with absolute certainty that it would have been child's play for me to release some of the bottle's contents. Nobody could have heard the material escape during the noise of the bombardment. What do you think of that?"

Rhodan's masklike face relaxed. From beneath the thick rimmed helmet a furrowed brow became partially visible. Slowly came the rejoinder, "Klein, if you had made one careless movement, you'd no longer be alive. I have a portable radioscope detector, which revealed at once the bottles under your overalls. You can rest assured that you would never have managed even to reach the opening valve with your little finger. Do you get me?"

Klein grinned in embarrassment. "Good," he snorted. "You knew about it all along. But I did not. Will you believe me that we did not intend for a single moment to blow that infernal stuff into your dome? I came here only to discuss things with you undisturbed."

"It is after 4 A.M. now. When you return they will ask you what you were doing here such a long time. Is that logical?"

"Absolutely. I can invent some plausible excuse. About the fictitious underground movement that supposedly wants to give you support in reaching your goals."

"And what do you really want?" asked Rhodan slowly. His eyes were burning.

Klein felt his calmness return. He could appreciate the human greatness of this man who was standing practically singlehanded against the massed forces of the world. "I am impressed by the integrity of your goals," he declared shortly. "We have already discussed this point once before. I see no justification for wanting to remove you as the Third Power. The outbreak, of the atomic war, which you foiled just in the nick of time, convinced me 100 percent of your honesty. You effected the unity of mankind. You made a dream come true that so far had seemed unattainable. I personally have always been convinced that only a threat coming from outside our planet would bring about an amalgamation of all nations. Ideological differences among the world's governments have become unimportant now. You are instead the focal point of the threat. Even religious differences have been removed overnight. People have started to think rationally, but they will stop doing so the moment you cease to exist. Can you believe me that I have experienced so much more as an officer of the IIA than an ordinary human being? Working for the secret service was a dirty job. We—that means Kosnow, Li and I—have arrived at the conclusion that you must continue to survive as the Third Power. These are our motivations in a nutshell."

Rhodan did not stop to think for long. Klein's intentions appeared to be quite clear; yet he overlooked one significant fact: The end of the Third Power he admired and found desirable was rapidly approaching.

Rhodan looked worriedly toward the sickbay. In a few short hours his daily report to Thora was due—and Khrest was still in his inexplicable cataleptic state.

"You must do something," urged Klein. "I have learned from a reliable source that three spaceships blasted off from Earth several hours ago. I don't know the exact time and place, but I do know their destination. These rocket ships were launched to the moon in order to attack your lunar base with a new kind of 'cold' atom bomb. You simply must do something."

Reginald Bell's fists were closed tightly around the narrow back of his chair. Rhodan's mouth was twisted in a wry smile, his eyes full of doubt. "Three moonrockets?" Rhodan's voice sounded skeptical. "Do you realize what you are saying? No atomic engine is able to start now on Earth—you can take my word for it."

"That's right, not from Earth. But beyond the outer limit of the antineutron belt. Secret experiments and measurements in the upper atmosphere were conducted, which show that the Arkonides' strange antineutron field extends only to a height of about seventy miles."

With a deep groan Klein sat down on a stool His knees were trembling. "So you had no idea about that planned lunar attack? The Western Bloc, the East and the Asiatic Federation have each launched one spaceship. The first and second stages are powered with chemical fuel. As soon as they reached an altitude of seventy miles the nuclear chemical aggregates began to take over. You made a serious mistake, Major Rhodan! This is why I have come here. Forget all the questioning to find out the why and wherefore of my actions. The only thing that matters now is to safeguard the existence of your moon base!"

Bell moistened his lips. His face had turned ashen. Even Rhodan grasped the back of a chair in front of him, as if searching for some kind of support.

"Tell us everything, please," he urged roughly. "What has happened? But report everything in detail, will you!"

Indeed, Klein did not spare them any of the details. He started with the conference in Greenland, then proceeded to a description of the Catalyst H bomb and its workings, which were easily comprehended by Rhodan.

Thus had come about the very thing he had always feared.

Klein finished his report by relating the tremendous job that had been accomplished by the mightiest electronic brain on Earth. As he fell silent, they became aware again of the dull pounding of the nonstop barrage. The Arkonide reactor was shining brightly in a light blue hue. It looked frightening. Rhodan racked his brain in desperation, trying to picture what malfunctions might be taking place inside the machine. Only Khrest could supply the answer, provided it was not too late for even that. What good would it do to know the why and how if the point of no return had already been reached! Rhodan was convinced of the imminent breakdown of the reactor.

Before Rhodan began to reply to Klein's account, he directed the psychoradiator toward the two other visitors. Kosnow and Li awoke instantly. A few brief explanations sufficed to bring them up to date.

"Abstain from any questions and complaints," they heard him say in their helmets' loudspeaker system. "Captain Klein has supplied me with all the necessary information. Okay, let's be quick about it."

He pointed toward the reactor. "Look at this! This bluish glow is not normal. I'm afraid that we have reached the end of our tether."

Klein shook his head in protest. His eyes, full of disbelief, were firmly fixed on the tall man near him. Rhodan continued with a bitter smile, "The Arkonides' transmitter is out of order, quite likely because of the strong ground tremors. Thus, it has become impossible for us to reestablish the disrupted radio communication with the moon. Unless Khrest is awake by 8 tomorrow morning, I'll be forced to surrender to the enemy forces, or at least I shall have to ask for an armistice. You can't begin to imagine what horrible fate lies in store for mankind if any evil should befall our sick visitor. Please, hold back all your questions. Things are too complicated to be explained thoroughly in a few moments."

"But what about the three nuclear bombers of the power

blocs!" groaned Kosnow. "Can they still be rendered harmless? And what will happen to their crews if your people on the moon base should answer this threat to their survival by a counterattack?"

"Let's hope that things will be handled as humanely as possible," declared Rhodan. "The woman commander of the moon base, though, is the one who will have to decide how to deal with the potential aggressors from earth."

"And if they should drop their bombs?" inquired Li Tschai-tung excitedly. "What chances will your garrison on the moon base have? Will they be able to defend themselves properly?"

Rhodan tried hard not to give any indication of the storm raging in him. He had an overwhelming desire to be left alone as soon as possible. These three men must not find too much about the situation. He particularly wanted to spare them the devastating effect that truth would now have on their belief in their own mission.

"Your assumption is right, that a cold nuclear fusion can not be stopped by an antineutron field. But they certainly have other means on the moon to render ineffective these three rockets with their deadly cargo. Don't worry about that. But before you leave, Klein, I have a request to make."

Captain Klein stood up. His face seemed gray and worn. He was aware that something was amiss. Bell could not hide his excitement.

Rhodan glanced at his watch. "Will you listen for my radio call at 8 A.M. sharp? I'll try to do my best to repair the sender by then. If I don't succeed, I see no alternative but to give up in order to prevent a catastrophe. If it is within your power, try to arrange for a cease fire. Send negotiators for a truce, gain time. But most urgently, see to it that this constant bombardment is stopped at once. Do you think you can manage that?"

Rhodan's eyes seemed to burn in their sockets. The Chinese interjected in too casual a manner, "Sir, you don't know my people! Before General Tai-tiang will stop the shooting you will have to remove the energy barrier around your encampment. If you simply request a truce, he will not go along with you. His suspicions will be aroused, and he will assume that this is nothing but a maneuver to win time to carry out some necessary repairs. There are some excellent psychologists in our command bunkers. Don't underestimate them. We can proceed only step by step, as you surely must know."

Klein nodded in agreement.

Rhodan lowered his head. "Okay, then wait for my radio call. If it doesn't arrive by 8 at your base, that will mean that we could manage things successfully. But if I should call you, will you then act as quickly as possible?"

"This reactor will keep on working for months on end," stammered Klein with hopeful zest. "Why do you want to throw in the towel so fast? This barrage is bound to cease sometime soon. They are already experiencing a lot of difficulties with fresh supplies from the rear. Six thousand guns need an incredible amount of ammunition. Try to hold out another day!"

"You don't fully understand what is going on here," Rhodan informed him. "If it were up to us, we would simply carry on until the machine failed. But there is another potential danger that I must avoid at all costs. If the commander of the moon base calls for the daily report without getting a reply from us, and if in addition to that she notices we are under constant fire, she will lose her temper. Then God have mercy on us down here on Earth! Do you understand now why I can't risk this?"

They understood. Rhodan accompanied the three men back to the protective screen perimeter. Before taking leave and having the protective earpad helmets returned to him, Rhodan said warmly, "Thank you, Klein. You meant well. I'm sorry to have to disappoint you in your high expectations. But some miracle might still happen. In that case, please act instantly and call Nevada Fields for an immediate cease fire. Have General Pounder affirm this by a broadcast. But to be on the safe side, will you also inform Allan D. Mercant that no finger must be laid on the alien Khrest. Otherwise, the debacle will be unavoidable. He must not be detained by anyone, do you understand?"

The circuits of the screen's structure were switched, and within an interval of three seconds the men had left the energy dome. As soon as they had reached the outside, Rhodan raced back to the tent.

"Those guys will get into trouble," he was informed by Reginald Bell. "They forgot their cylinders with the bacterial cultures."

"We have taken that into consideration. They will declare that they have discharged their poisonous cargo into our atmosphere within the dome. If we stay healthy despite that, they will be free of blame. After all, we might have means to fend off such bacteriological warfare. The Third Power is capable of everything. Let them believe that!"

The sarcastic grin with which Rhodan concluded his words caused Reginald Bell to break out in loud curses. He looked up at his commander in anguish.

"Come along now," Perry said.

Once Rhodan and Bell had arrived inside the temporary sickbay, both medics were tuned in to their intercom system. Dr. Manoli and Dr. Haggard looked exhausted. Both had reached the limit of nervous endurance.

"It is 4:55 now," stated Rhodan. He glanced slowly around the room. Khrest was resting motionless on his cot.

"Klein did not know exactly when the three moon rockets started. But it is safe to assume that there will be atomic fireworks on the moon today and without the slightest risk for the people down here on Earth. The moon is too far away for that."

"What is your opinion about the whole deal? You seem to have some idea." Reginald Bell's hands were tense as they grasped Rhodan's arms. "Spill it! What's going to happen?"

"Thora will ignore the threat from the three moon rockets in her morbid arrogance. She will assume she is able to counteract any nuclear reaction with the help of a normal protective screen and the antineutron field. Even if I could restore communication with her immediately and warn her, she would choose to disregard it. That means that the destruction of the space sphere is only a matter of time now."

"You are imagining the impossible," stammered Bell. "That's out of question! That giant ship is indestructible."

"Only under the proper circumstances is it invulnerable. If they had a terrestrial crew on board instead of their apathetic Arkonides, I would not be worried at all. But they will neglect to take the most elementary precautions. I am very pessimistic. A catalyst H bomb will develop an energy output of 100 megatons of TNT. I would not care to be at the center of the ball of gas resulting from such a nuclear reaction. A terrible sun will rise over the space sphere unless something is done by its crew in time. Dr. Haggard. . . . !"

The physician responded with a startled movement. Then he slowly lifted his head. His eyes locked with Rhodan's steely, dominating glance. The doctor's posture stiffened as if in anticipated protest.

"Dr. Haggard, will you now try to rouse Khrest from his strange sleep? Eric, you will assist your colleague. It is senseless to wait any longer. You must risk everything now."

Haggard felt like resisting, but the longer he gazed into those burning eyes the weaker grew his will to resist.

"As you wish, Major!" he replied in a monotonous voice.

Rhodan turned away. It was 5 o'clock sharp. Outside the shooting continued with undiminished intensity.

Far beyond the protective energy bell the three men were welcomed back by officers of the defense.

Captain Klein made his report. ". . . and we arrived at the conclusion that Rhodan seemed to believe in our explanations. The three pressurized containers remained behind inside the cordoned-off area. Kosnow and I managed to open the valves, but Li had no chance to do so. We assume though that two charges should be enough to achieve the desired effect."

A helicopter transported the men to the disinfection center. This caused intense agony for Klein. What would happen if the physicians should think it necessary to keep them in quarantine for some time! . . .

At about the same time the commanding officer aboard the Western Bloc's moon rocket sent a last message back to Earth. His rocket had been racing through the black night sky for the last fifteen hours as the spearhead of a small armada, sent by the three blocs to attack the threatening moon base. Four men manned each of the three giant rockets that carried their death dealing cargoes of the catalyst H bombs.

CHAPTER SIX

THEY SAT in silent apathy on their provisional seating arrangements in the big tent. They gave the appearance, at least, that the incessant bombardment outside no longer mattered.

The sun had risen two hours earlier. The brilliant sunlight had extinguished the will-o'-the-wisps of the innumerable explosions that had irritated their eyes in the dark of the night. Still the roaring thunder remained. The energy dome was swaying in a strange rhythm that could lead any moment to a final collapse of the protective structure.

Since 5 A.M. the two physicians had endeavored to awaken the alien patient from his morbid slumber. Partial successes had been accomplished, when Khrest began to breathe faster and slight twitchings were observed on his eyelids. But soon these weak symptoms of hope had been dissipated.

Finally, toward 7 o'clock, Dr. Frank Haggard had resorted to the most efficacious modern psychostimulator. This drug directly affected the waking center in man's brain. In addition, it caused a very strong increase of circulatory reactions and nervous reflexes. Psycho-Stimulin was the last means that the desperate medics had at their disposal.

Mankind had united surprisingly fast in face of the common threat from outside their home planet. They knew, though, that the world's safety would not be endangered by the bomb carrying moon rockets. In case of a launching failure none of the catalyst H bombs would ever have been able to explode.

But there had been no accidents. All three spaceships had roared off into their element, after the *Stardust II* had proved that it was possible to pass through the antineutron zone.

Freedom I, the manned space station of the West, had taken over the remote control steering of both the Western Bloc's rocket and that of the Asiatic Federation. The Eastern Bloc ship was directed by the excellently equipped satellite of the Eastern powers.

Twelve men, astronaut soldiers of the three mighty power blocs of the world, had received their orders on how to carry out their mission. Now First Lieutenant Freyt from the leading *Stardust II* reported, "Started braking acceleration. Engines working satisfactory. All well aboard ship. Keep your fingers crossed."

Three bombardiers were calculating when they would release their bombs. "In approximately three hours," estimated Captain Nyssen aloud on board the *Stardust II.* Then he was hit by the powerful grip of the G forces.

Khrest reacted to the drug like a man to a cup of coffee. Thus Haggard had decided to give him a second injection, five minutes after the first, but this time intravenously.

It was 7:48. Perry Rhodan glanced once again at the patient before he reached slowly for the portable radio transmitter. At this very moment the Arkonide sat bolt upright, as if an inner power had shot a sudden surge of energy through his body.

Rhodan stopped in midmotion. A man's groan became audible in the earphones. It was Dr. Haggard, who had followed his patient's incredible reaction in speechless confusion. Never before had Khrest's constitution manifested so clearly that the patient had not been born on this planet.

What Dr. Manoli had predicted now came true. Either Khrest would sink into an everdeepening slumber from which he would never awake or he would wake up in a reflex action to an instant state of full awareness and clear thinking.

Khrest was now fully awake—there was no doubt about it. His first action was a painful grimace. His narrow, emaciated hand then moved to his temples.

Rhodan grasped the meaning of this gesture before any of his friends. With a quick movement he pulled the sound-proof helmet, with its built in communication system, over the alien's head. The instrument had already been switched on.

"Khrest, can you hear me? Do you understand me?" Rhodan's voice was so shrill that Bell could hardly recognize it as his friend's. It was shrieking and gave evidence of a tremendous nervous tension.

Rhodan, however, knew that he did not have any time to spare for long winded explanations. If Khrest had regained full awareness, they must begin to act at once.

"I . . . I am listening," Khrest's voice came feebly over the speakers. "This noise . . . what is—!"

"Later," Rhodan interrupted. "You'll get all necessary explanations. We have finally managed to rouse you from your deep, extended sleep. You are cured, Khrest! You are no longer suffering from leukemia. But now we are forced to act immediately. We have been under heavy bombardment for many hours. The reactor is glowing in a light blue hue. I am afraid of an imminent failure. In addition to that, the transmitter is no longer functioning because of the tremendous, prolonged ground tremors. We. . . ."

No one could have foreseen the effect of these words on Khrest. What under similar circumstances would have been most harmful disclosures for any human being were nothing but the best therapy for the biologically divergent organism of the alien.

Khrest sat up abruptly. Suddenly his dim eyes grew alert and bright; but his face became painfully contorted. He had completely grasped the situation just a few seconds after awaking from a deathlike trance.

The two medics were horrified. Manoli, who had been prepared to assist in any arising emergency, soon realized that his fears had been unfounded. Totally exhausted, he laid down his hypodermic syringe, which he had held ready for a booster shot, all the while shaking his head in utter disbelief. Haggard, on the other hand, observed silently and with the utmost concentration.

"Switch off the reactor at once!" commanded Khrest, loud and strong. "Danger of overheating. Turn it off!"

Rhodan regained his composure. He could react calmly and instantaneously, even under stress. He understood the fear expressed in the alien's eyes.

"That would mean the end for us, Khrest," he declared briefly. "It is 7:55. Thora will call us in five minutes. The reactor will hold out till then. If Thora intervenes right away, everything will be all right. All we need to do now is repair the transmitter. Can you do this?"

"In five minutes?" stammered the alien. He was looking around for the instrument, which was next to his cot. "What is the matter with it? It can't possibly fail. Have you switched on 'automatic repair'?"

Rhodan's face changed color. Reginald Bell muttered a strong comment. Khrest's breathing became labored. His heart seemed to be under increasing stress, and he was gasping for air.

"What about that switch for 'automatic repair'?" Rhodan groaned, his hands closed into tight fists. "I don't know anything about it. Which switch?"

"The robot microautomatic," returned Khrest. "It automatically repairs any damage occurring at the connections. Storage batteries or any other part of the set are indestructible, provided that the vacuum inside the instrument remains intact."

Rhodan moved quickly over to the cube shaped apparatus. It had no visible connection to any source of current. Only the antenna, with its fluorescent terminal knob, indicated that this was a transmitter.

The oval shaped, concave screen remained empty. While Bell stared at the stranger full of tortured feelings of self-recrimination, Rhodan pushed the instrument closer to the alien's reach. He did not waste any unnecessary comments.

"Proceed with the switchover, quickly!" he urged Bell. "We had no idea that this has an automatic repair system. We have three minutes left."

The alien scientist reacted immediately. He had again comprehended the situation. He did not need any explanations. The switchover to automatic repair was simplicity itself. Rhodan closed his eyes to hide his amazement. A green light symbol appeared on the screen.

"Repair is proceeding," panted Khrest. "We must wait now. Show me the reactor. It must be turned off."

Bell moved the dividing curtain aside. Khrest's reddish eyes widened in horror at the spectacle that presented itself.

"Approximately half an hour of your time, but not more than that!" he stated. "The instrument has been working with an overload for several hours, which necessitated an increased nuclear reaction output. The thermal transformers are operating at maximum values. How was this possible?"

Rhodan began to give brief explanations. Khrest's comments were more complicated. Rhodan grasped the gist of his explanation, but that was all. Rarely had he felt as helpless as at this moment.

The green light subsided at 7:59. Rhodan turned on the set with trembling hands. Flickering light patterns raced across the screen. Static noises became audible. Then suddenly sound and picture came on with such clarity that Dr. Haggard was reminded of the similar spontoneous awakening of the Arkonide scientist. The robot automatic had worked perfectly. Probably the damage was nothing but a loose connection because of the constant ground tremors.

Khrest and Rhodan were standing in front of the scintillating screen. The set was a miracle of a superior technology.

Commander Perry Rhodan had thought of every eventuality except for what took place shortly thereafter. The brief report he intended to give became superfluous, since the shrill voice of the highly excited woman made any rational comment impossible.

Thora, the woman commander of the gigantic spaceship on the moon, was beside herself, her beautiful face glowing with fury.

". . . ask you what has happened," came hissing like a whip from the invisible loudspeaker system.

Rhodan comprehended with lightning speed that she must have been talking for quite some time already. This meant that she must have been trying to establish communication before the repair of the sender had been completed.

"Listen to me, Thora! For heaven's sake will you just listen to me!" he yelled in reply, trying to outshout her.

"The reactor has turned blue. The field is going to collapse unless you immediately—!"

"Where is Khrest?" she interrupted, still screaming at the top of her lungs. "I have been overgenerous with you. I have come to the end of my patience. Don't bother to explain, Major Rhodan! If anything untoward should happen to Khrest I'll abandon you ruthlessly and attack you with all means at my disposal. I'll simply annihilate you!"

Rhodan stepped aside. He could hardly control his emotions. Bell's face seemed frozen in an icy grin. Both friends listened to the conversation that ensued between the two Arkonides. Although they could not understand anything, they were still able to see that Thora's excitement subsided.

Thora calmed down, but before Rhodan managed to speak to her again she cut the communication. Rhodan pressed down on the red switch but in vain.

He turned around, his face flushed with anger. "Your people react in a most peculiar fashion!" he remarked bitingly. His hands were jerking convulsively. "May I ask what further actions the scion of the Almighty Dynasty of the Arkonides is contemplating?"

Khrest smiled faintly. He was resting quietly on his couch. "She has already left the moon base in one of our biggest auxiliary vessels," came the startling reply. "She called us a few minutes before the agreed upon time, after the robot instruments had registered the heavy bombardment. She is deeply worried. Major Rhodan, you should try to understand our position. Unless she intervenes at once with the superstrength machines of the auxiliary vessel, we are all lost. Therefore, it would be to your own advantage to refrain from provoking punitive measures against mankind, which you represent. Avoid at all costs that I should fall into the hands of any terrestrial power group. That was the condition under which she agreed to come to your aid. Thora will arrive here in ten minutes."

"*In ten minutes!*" was Rhodan's amazed rejoinder. "In ten minutes from the moon to Earth, including the difficult landing maneuver?"

Khrest was breathing normally again. The two medics

were administering various drugs and checking all vital signs constantly.

"Incredible," muttered Dr. Haggard. "He is over the hump. If I only could have foreseen such a fantastic response, I would have injected the Psycho-Stimulin much sooner. How do you feel, Khrest?"

"That's a very important question. But it will have to wait. Mine is more urgent right now!" interjected Rhodan with icy tones. Khrest seemed to be slightly startled. He focused his attention on the tall man and kept him under a continued critical scrutiny.

"Have you explained to Thora that three new type nuclear bomber spaceships are on their way to the moon? Of course not! You did not give me a chance to inform you about the impending danger to your base on the moon. And this wild woman up there preferred to interrupt the connection before I could even warn you. Perhaps you can't even consider the possibility that humans could think of some way to get around the antineutron field, which anyhow is limited in its effectiveness. Unless Thora acts at once, your beautiful space sphere will be atomized in the center of a white hot ball formed by three heavy H bombs. And don't say these reactions cannot take place! They certainly will! My fellow scientists in the Western Bloc have developed a process of cold fusion on the catalytic basis of mesons. These three bombs won't give a damn about Thora's antineutron field. Khrest, I have never been more serious than now! Get in touch with Thora immediately and make sure that she proceeds with the necessary countermeasures without delay."

Khrest had turned ashen. "Cold fusion?" he echoed faintly. "We will locate the three Earth ships in time and render their deadly cargo harmless. Our cruiser's robot automatic brain will carry out all defensive measures even without Thora's assistance."

"Of course, Khrest!" Rhodan's compliment had a trace of sarcasm in it. "The question is, though, whether the robot brain has been properly programmed. Your cruiser's positronic brain has been instructed to deal with primitive creatures, isn't that so? Therefore, it is forced to ignore any defensive measures because of its purely mechanical logic, which would not have been the case if the positronic memory bank had been correctly programmed. The brain is bound to underestimate the danger, since it is unable to think on an individual basis. Not a single one of its calculations will take into account catalytic superbombs with a yield of 300 million tons of TNT. The robot brain *must* act wrong! It has been adjusted to the values of our first lunar landing expedition and will accordingly disrupt the remote steering control signals, erect a normal antineutron field and in addition to that perhaps construct a protective energy screen. But you can't expect anything more from the automatic brain, since its built in mechanical logic will not allow it to undertake any steps beyond the bare exigencies. Why shoot sparrows with a big cannon if a buckshot gun will do just as well! Do you get the analogy? Khrest, do call Thora this instant! She absolutely must turn back. The three spaceships might drop their bombs any moment now. You can't afford to wait any longer! Please, get in touch with her and don't delay!"

The Arkonide was lying motionless on his cot. Only his eyes seemed to be alive. Something began to stir in them—disbelief. This was more than even this most tolerant representative of an incredibly superior technology could comprehend. How could the weapons of a race that had reached only intelligence level D be so effective?

"Wait a minute, please," he whispered. "I am still feeling quite weak. Besides, I cannot reach Thora just now. Our transmitter here can establish communication only with our research cruiser on the lunar base."

"Then won't you at least try to get in touch with one of the members of the crew!" Rhodan demanded in desperation. "Khrest, you don't seem to understand how serious things are! Your human enemies are going to attack you with all they have at their disposal. Do something now!"

"Nothing can be done. It is hopeless," came the alien's dejected reply. "Don't you realize that our crew will be lying in front of their simulator screens, admiring some new masterwork? Nobody will pay the slightest attention to any incoming signal."

Rhodan gasped, completely shocked. He barely refrained

from making some choice comments. This alien race had reached the bitter end, there was no doubt about it.

Slowly, he went toward the exit of the tent. His gaze serached the blue morning sky above the Gobi Desert. Some monstrosity should soon be making its appearance up there, according to Khrest. Rhodan could well imagine what the Arkonides meant by an "auxiliary vessel." Twenty or more terrestrial rockets would easily find accommodation inside.

An infernal roar arose. Rhodan closed his eyes and moaned softly. An alien power began to unfold a display of its super-strength.

CHAPTER SEVEN

IT WAS SENSELESS to attempt to take cover. The narrow observation slits of the reinforced concrete bunkers were changed into organ pipes, emitting hellish howls.

Compared with this inferno, a hurricane would seem like a mild breeze. In the last moment Thora had given up her intention of destroying the cordon of troops encircling the energy dome. Nevertheless, it was necessary from her point of view to teach a lesson to these "primitive creatures."

Khrest, of course, could understand Thora's motivation. But it was almost incomprehensible for Rhodan why she had to unleash this horrendous storm. As a representative of a galactic empire, she had been deeply humiliated by the constant bombardment of the energy wall she had erected around the *Stardust I*. Her emotions were identical with those experienced by the old time colonial officers of the planet Earth, who considered any revolt of the underdeveloped dark skinned colonial population a blasphemy directed toward the white skinned ruling class.

The mighty space sphere was hovering close to the vaulted dome of the energy bell. It was beyond Rhodan's imagination how Thora had caused this hurricane's fury. But then, what could poor Earthlings grasp of the intricate workings of such a superior alien civilization and its machinery!

The enormous waves of pressure swept outward. The fire of the innumerable batteries died down so fast that it was hard to see how it ever could have constituted a threat to the besieged inside the dome. The men of the Asiatic elite divisions could barely manage to cling desperately to any hold inside their excellent trenches until the additional effect of null gravity made itself felt.

The sudden release from the gravitational pull of mother Earth robbed men and any nonalive matter of its foothold on the ground. More than 150,000 soldiers rose, whirling like dead autumn leaves out of the trenches, toward the open desert.

Heavy guns and stacks of ammunition presented a much larger target area. They were seized by the howling waves of pressure and torn loose like toys.

That was the only weapon used by Thora. Most probably she considered it rather primitive. Besides, it was a rather humane weapon, as Rhodan had reluctantly to admit.

The nonstop barrage of gunfire had been silenced abruptly. There was simply nothing left on the ground still capable of shooting.

Only the strong ground bunkers could withstand this inferno. Any other structures or objects that had not been fastened down tightly were pulled up in the air and then gently deposited outside the powerful antigravity field, where the raging hurricane, too, had spent its strength. Thus, men and materials were gathered peacefully together in a safe zone. They could still see the energy dome, but their gun emplacements had all disappeared.

The moment Captain Klein felt firm ground under his feet again and began to overcome his nausea, he observed the collapse of the energy screen. A roaring structure descended slowly into the formerly cordoned off area. Occasionally one of the bunkers opened fire with small arms, but the bullets fell far short.

From then on Klein no longer bothered looking at his

watch. The critical moment had come and gone. Now it had become quite superfluous for Rhodan to ask for a truce.

Klein assisted the Chinese commander in chief to push aside the shattered remnants of a small card table. Only then could Lieutenant General Tai-tiang free himself and stand up again.

Outside, the sun was shining brightly. The organ-like roaring had completely died down. But inside the concrete bunkers there reigned total chaos. Men picked themselves up off the floor, some cursing, others too shocked to utter a sound. Several scientists looked about in a puzzled but inquisitive manner. Never before had Klein been able to observe so easily the full range of human emotions on either pale or flushed faces.

Colonel Donald Cretcher, liaison officer of the Western Defense, came tramping up from the depths of the command bunker, bleeding profusely from his forehead. A brief glance around the room was all he needed to assess the situation. A few words by Cretcher accomplished what Klein had hoped for so fervently.

"Sir, under these circumstances we deem it advisable to cease fire immediately. It is absolutely senseless to remount our attack."

"Who?" stammered Tai-tiang. "The batteries . . . ?"

"Have been torn loose from their positions. Panic all along the line. A little while before this unknown spaceship landed near the *Stardust I*, I received an important message from our headquarters in Greenland. We—that means my colleagues and myself—have arrived at the conclusion that we should bide our time now, rather than act."

Major Butaan, former officer of the Asiatic Federation Secret Service, did not waste any unnecessary remarks. He barked roughly, "Cease fire at once! I'll be responsible for everything."

This made Tai-tiang finally realize that he had lost. There was no protesting the orders given by Major Butaan.

General Tai-tiang staggered across the room to the wall. In a daze he perceived through the observation windows the horrifying spectacle outside. There was the energy dome again, but bigger and mightier than before.

The first reports arrived from the various commando posts

via radio. The cordon around the *Stardust I* no longer existed. The military detachments were in the process of complete dissolution.

Klein rubbed his sweating palms dry on his trousers. He and Kosnow exchanged a brief glance. The faint grin of the Eastern Defense officer told everything. Rhodan had won . . . at least for the time being!

She arrived displaying the grandiose power of the "Great Empire" and with the insulting arrogance of a goddess.

Rhodan's stature seemed to shrink next to hers. His remarks became futile, and his arguments were simply ignored. Her reply consisted of a momentary frown, full of exasperation.

At this point the commander apparently resigned himself and with a very odd smile followed her figure, which soon disappeared through the exit door of the tent.

Reginald Bell could not comprehend what was happening to him. Full of fury and indignation, he was struggling helplessly in the steely grip of a robot soldier that had just emerged from the huge auxiliary vessel. And that robot was only one of a small troop of automated humanoid war machines.

The so-called auxiliary vessel had turned out to be something far different from the normal human concept of a small space nodule to be used in case of emergency. It was a gigantic structure with a diameter of almost 200 feet, with mighty engines and power stations.

It represented an exact duplicate in miniature of the original Arkonide research cruiser that the *Stardust I* crew had encountered on the moon. Yet this "auxiliary vessel" surpassed any earthly spaceship in dimensions and, of course, in equipment.

From the distance the Arkonide robots were similar to a teeming stream of ants. Closely following each other, they left the gaping air lock in the lower part of the space sphere.

Rhodan could distinguish several varying models of the automatons. The robot soldiers had two pairs of many jointed arms. Two of these limbs apparently served exclusively as weapons. Rhodan had no doubt that any of these machines was the equivalent of a full company of human soldiers. Still, this was a difficult notion to accept. To realize the full extent of the robot soldiers' efficiency, one had to see them in action. A demonstration was indispensable for the human brain before it was willing to admit the unquestioned superiority of a nonhuman technology.

A sharp command caused Bell to cease struggling. As soon as he complied with the order the steely claws of the machine relaxed their hold on him.

A monotonous tinny voice issued from the invisible loudspeaker inside the robot. "You are requested to remain calm and stop any resistance. You are not to leave this spot!"

Reginald staggered over toward Rhodan. In the meantime the upper polar dome of the spaceship began to light up and construct an energy screen, glowing in a deep violet hue. This convinced Rhodan that the *Stardust's* crew need no longer fear any danger from their terrestrial enemies.

Beyond the energy screen's perimeter there reigned absolute silence. With growing alarm Rhodan kept wondering what the fate of the Asiatic divisions might have been. A slight moan came from Bell's direction. Rhodan's face relaxed as he turned toward him.

"Don't melt your ice, friend!" he said emphatically. "Keep it cool." With narrowed eyes he peered over toward the tent where Thora was probably being brought up to date about Khrest's state of health.

"Our most revered lady friend is just about to commit the biggest blunder in her life. Well, let her! Unless I'm greatly mistaken she'll be a bundle of raw nerves about ten hours from now; just like any other woman who has been hurt to the quick. Don't say another word. Leave everything to me. We'll wait here till she comes out of the tent again. That's all there is to it."

"I don't understand a darn thing you're saying, I assure you," replied Bell gruffly.

"She will be reduced to a nervous wreck," Rhodan continued with emphasis. "And she will be forced to pass on to us some of her superior knowledge, if she ever wants to see her home planet again. She will have no other alternative, in case the big research cruiser has really been totally destroyed. She is very near sighted. She is generally inclined to underestimate her opponents. She is going to be taught a bitter lesson, and that at the hands of people that she, in her incredible arrogance, regards as primitive and inferior."

A glimmer of understanding began to dawn in Bell's eyes. Now he realized the reasons behind Rhodan's strange behavior.

"I'm beginning to see the light," he said slowly. "You are convinced that the three moon rockets will score a hit, aren't you?"

"It looks like it," murmured Rhodan. "But don't let's discuss this any further now. She will be back here in a moment. Khrest has a much better grasp of the situation, particularly a more objective one."

Soon after, when the tall, slender woman came running out of the tent, she found both men sitting quietly on the ground. Breathing heavily and shivering because of the the insufficient warmth that this planet's weak sun was generating for one of her race, she stopped near them.

Rhodan looked up with studied equanimity and an enigmatic expression in his eyes. She was panting with great effort, her chest heaving. The first signs of uneasiness were showing in her exquisite face, which was of an unearthly beauty.

"Hello. How are you?" inquired Rhodan in deliberately calm tones. "May I thank you most sincerely for your help. Khrest will be able to leave with you. He is cured. His last traces of weakness should soon disappear with plenty of rest and the proper diet. There is nothing to hold you here any longer. You can depart any time it suits you."

Thora's whole body seemed to stiffen. She looked down at the man sitting so relaxed on the ground, her face displaying a mixture of fear, perplexity and indignation. Her voice came shrilly, rapidly firing away at him, full of accusatic : "Why was I not informed at once about the impending attack? I have—"

"You have behaved like a hysterical schoolgirl," Perry interrupted. His eyes were aflame. "You broke off radio communication with us before I had a chance to make my report to you and to explain the reasons for our temporary radio silence. I can give you only one good piece of advice —get back to your moon base as fast as you can, and let's hope they leave you enough time to reach your research space cruiser. Have your instruments located the three foreign intruders? Well, don't stand there like a deaf mute. Did you get any word from your position finders?"

She nodded an affirmation. The pallor of her face intensified. Her hands started to tremble.

Rhodan got to his feet. "And what countermeasures have you taken?"

Thora did not answer his question but instead began to stammer, "Come along with us—please, do come along to our moon base! When were the rockets launched? What kind of armament do they have on board? Khrest mentioned something about a—"

"Meson catalytic bomb," Rhodan finished for her. "A fusion weapon that will not react to your antineutron screen. Have you at least made provisions for any eventualities and taken care of the necessary defensive programming instructions to your robot brain? Any commander of a terrestrial spaceship would have made sure of that."

Thora did not waste a second. She did not even bother to give any explanations, which told Rhodan clearly that she must have neglected to take any precautionary measures whatsoever.

She was running as fast as she could, and Bell and Rhodan stayed with her. A thought crossed Rhodan's mind while he tried to keep up with her fast pace. He was struck by the similarity of their current situation and the Bible story of David and Goliath. Haughtiness on the one hand and lack of foresight on the other could lead to the destruction of the supergiant space sphere by the feeble but alert young opponent. This was particularly true since the deep apathy of the alien crew would, judging by previous experiences, prevent them from taking quick action against any threatening danger.

The gravity elevator deposited them directly in the control center of the auxiliary vessel. Thora had traveled to Earth in it all alone. She explained nervously that this was a fully automated vehicle that could be directed by any living being capable of individual thinking.

Rhodan looked around and began to feel dizzy. The complicated instrument panels of the *Stardust* seemed, in comparison with these fantastic installations, like a primitive native's log canoe compared with an aircraft carrier of the U.S. Navy.

There were no launching preparations with long-drawn-out procedures. The leap into space occurred as abruptly, as matter of factly and without any noticeable transition, as if an experienced driver had simply started his car. Never before had anything made Rhodan realize so sharply the gaping abyss between the Arkonide level of knowledge and that of Earth.

Thora directed the spaceship's drive by a few slight manipulations that seemed simplicity itself. Innumerable robot instruments began to function at a simple touch of a lever. Rhodan was suddenly startled by the roar of the power unit that had started up. Lights were flickering across screens, and panels glowed in soft illumination. Rhodan was all set to experience the well-known unpleasant effects of sudden high acceleration, but nothing happened. The sphere simply lifted off the ground in vertical drive at tremendous speed.

The ground fell back beneath them. Before Rhodan relaxed his tense posture, the better to withstand the anticipated effects of high G pressures, he could already see the curvature of the Earth. The Pacific Ocean became visible, and then the outline of the West Coast lay beneath them like a design on a giant globe.

The shrill howling and whistling of tortured air masses subsided. In a few moments they had left behind them the last traces of the Earth's atmosphere. Space opened up ahead of them.

Rhodan turned around. Reginald Bell was crouching with an air of total consternation in one of the high backed chairs, which apparently could not even be folded over to form a horizontal couch. Perry judged accordingly that there was no problem connected with the effects of sudden acceleration as far as the Arkonides were concerned. He estimated that the ship must have been accelerating in excess of 1,000 G's. Nevertheless, he could not feel the slightest discomfort.

"How on Earth do they manage that?" wheezed Bell with trembling lips. "For heaven's sake, how is this possible? We are racing straight into the moon. Thora. . . . !"

The last word came like a scream. Rhodan whirled around. The moon's globe was fully visible on the front side screen. Seconds later only partial sections of its surface could be contained on the picture screen.

The thunder from the unbelievably powerful engines grew to an unbearable ear splitting level. White hot streams of fire leaped from the nozzle openings of the equatorial bulge. They shot out in the opposite direction from the drive. The Arkonides no longer needed to counteract their forward speed by turning the main engines around! Rhodan just could not believe his eyes. He was fighting with his rebelling mind against emotions coming from the unconscious. His reasoning told him that such things were impossible and beyond imagination.

He was taken with leisurely, meandering thoughts that could not be forced to focus on one firm viewpoint. Rhodan became a creature torn by divergent feelings.

He was torn out of his reveries when Thora called out sharply. Her hand jerked upward. On one of the other picture screens three glimmering dots became visible.

"The moon rockets!" said Bell. "They are now just above the lunar south pole!"

They were coasting in free fall. The automatic steering impulses had ceased as soon as the remote control stations on the manned satellites had initiated the first circular orbit of the *Stardust II*.

This had still caused a most fearful shock to Major Rhodan on his approach to the moon with the *Stardust I*. But First Lieutenant Freyt, Commanding Officer of the *Stardust II*, did not experience the slightest alarm when the remote control steering was abruptly discontinued.

The three rocketships remained exactly in their prescribed orbits. Nothing else happened that Freyt could interpret as defensive measures emanating from the alien moon base.

Captain Rod Nyssen took over the command after they had twice circled the moon from pole to pole. The ship's sighting mechanism was functioning with great precision. The automatic steering brains of the three rocket bombers constantly received new impulses via the commando unit of the *Stardust II*.

Nyssen waited until the light signal changed to red. A spherical structure appeared on the radar screen. Lieutenant Rickert, who was in charge of the optical direction finder, announced that the identification of their goal was established beyond a doubt. Lightning fast calculations of the computer stated the true dimensions of their target.

First Lieutenant Freyt proceeded to the last step of this desperate enterprise. "Commandant of *Stardust II* to escort vessels: target sighted, location fixed. Attention all bombardiers, watch for orders when to release bombs. Captain Nyssen, all clear."

Captain Nyssen was calmness itself. He counted aloud the last seconds. The automatic steering mechanisms built into the nuclear warheads were clicking away in the storerooms of the rocketships. Final corrections were made.

". . . three . . . two . . . one . . fire!" came Nyssen's order over the radiophone

A fire spewing missile left each of the rocketships. They were visible as bright flares for just a fraction of a second on the screens of the outside TV cameras; then they disappeared from sight as they zeroed in on their target like homing pigeons to their roost.

The automatic steering systems of the rocketships began to reverse the ships' direction almost immediately, and the roaring engines pulled them off-course at extremely high speeds.

All the lieutenant had in mind at this moment was to make a fast getaway. The detonations would be terrible. The ship raced off in a steep angle. Far below them, more than 500 miles away, the swivel mounted steering jets of the Rak missiles were already moving. Their aim had been automatically locked in tight, absolutely immovable.

A nuclear explosion in a vacuum must of necessity have an effect quite different from that within a dense atmosphere.

One of the main destructive effects, namely, the horrendous waves of pressure caused by the highly compressed, glowing hot air masses, would naturally not occur on the airless moon.

Since they lacked any experimental data about the radius of atomic effects in a vacuum, they had decided to detonate the heaviest H bombs upon impact on the target. Their aim was directly under ground zero, where the nuclear processes of the three missiles were scheduled to take place simultaneously.

Whatever was in the target's bull's-eye must therefore be enveloped by the inner gas ball of the three merging explosions and become not only pulverized by them but also vaporized by the ensuing temperature, comparable to that of a white hot sun.

Radioactive radiations had been considered as negligible, at least in this particular case. The effect of the pressure wave must decrease much faster in airless space than in a dense atmosphere. Practically, it would be limited to the area over which the gases could be expanded.

Thus, nobody had counted on the creation of an artificial sun. The white bluish ball appeared first like a pinpoint of intensely bright light, which expanded with incredible speed to a gigantic, fantastically brilliant formation.

Nothing like the infamous mushroom cloud developed. Instead, the south polar region of the moon was transformed into a boiling, evaporating crater, from which giant masses of rock were hurled skyward.

The steadily growing ball of energy, or primeval forces set free, could be observed even from the space stations circling the Earth. The white hot glowing gas formation had become so enormous that it stretched beyond the still recognizable horizon of the moon.

The Arkonide auxiliary vessel was rushing into the outer fringes of this awesome explosion. When it was over Rhodan could no longer remember what he had felt or thought during the few seconds their ship had penetrated and raced through this blazing hell.

He knew only that all of the space sphere's high capacity reactors had been switched over to the energy screens by their unbelievably fast functioning positronic control.

The vessel had been thrown off-course and hurled far out into space. Only there had the automatic control managed to stabilize it again.

Ten minutes had passed since the attack. The Arkonide sphere, as if motionless, stood in empty space. Thora was strangely quiet. With lifeless eyes she gazed at the picture screens that showed in all clarity the extent of the catastrophe. Somewhere in the center of this boiling witch's cauldron must have been the Arkonide research cruiser.

Rhodan waited a few minutes before he asked softly, "You are blaming yourself now, aren't you? Don't, please—it is senseless. Why don't you learn from my own race? I can't believe that your ship can have withstood this onslaught. But in any case you will have to wait until the reaction has died down."

For Rhodan, the utterly clear thinking man, devoid of any illusions, the Arkonide cruiser's destruction was an accepted fact. He was too much of a realist to cry over spilt atoms. It was not worthwhile for him even to waste any thought about things that could no longer be changed. He warned Thora, "Thora, don't think of retribution! Abandon your plans for reprisal. May I suggest that we land at once in the Gobi Desert? You can choose between undignified, caveman type vengeance or the exigencies of logical deliberation. Make your choice. Neither you nor Khrest would be helped in any way should you decide on a punitive action. And besides, I assure you, you would encounter serious difficulties from my side."

She looked down at the weapon in his hand. A bitter expression played around her full lips.

"I simply underestimated you, that's all," she replied in a monotonous voice. "Do you really believe that a Commander of the Great Imperium would go to pieces over a destroyed spaceship? Such things happen to us quite frequently. So what do you suggest?"

Rhodan knew then that he had finally won. The panicky actions of a frightened mankind had accomplished something that, although he did not agree with these actions in principle, he had considered in his innermost thoughts to be the basis for attaining a position of cosmic power.

Both Arkonides, Thora and Khrest, were definitely stranded now in this corner of the galaxy. There was no way back for them. With this in mind Rhodan declared thoughtfully, "Why don't you land first? I shall try to have the Third Power declared a sovereign state, fully recognized by all the nations of the world. Just leave that all to me."

She was a defeated person, crushed and helpless. Rhodan

knew it. A short hour later the space sphere touched ground again on the stony expanses of the Gobi Desert.

Far out in space, still at a great distance from their home planet, twelve men breathed easier. They were the crews of the three returning rocketships.

"I wish we were as far advanced as that!" whispered First Lieutenant Freyt, throwing a last glance at the video screens. "Did you see that racing comet? If only we were at their stage of progress—with ships like that the whole galaxy would be ours!"

PART TWO

TWILIGHT OF THE GODS

CHAPTER ONE

TOWARD NOON the roaring of the endless barrage grew weaker. Now there were only occasional detonations of heavy grenades exploding on the surface of the invisible energy screen; their strength was spent in producing brilliant flashes of lightning without achieving their intended effect.

Then complete silence followed.

The four men who were sitting in the former command center of the *Stardust I* looked at each other. Captain Reginald Bell sluggishly pushed aside the chessboard. "What is that supposed to mean?" he asked.

His chess partner looked regretfully at the chess figures that had been knocked over by Bell's negligent gesture, before he replied, shrugging his shoulders, "Your guess is as good as mine. Probably just a brief firing pause."

"After days and days of nonstop bombardment? I bet they must have a good reason to stop the shooting."

"That bet you are bound to win for sure," nodded the man sitting across from Bell. "There are always some reasons for everything." He pointed to the tumbled over chess figures. "By the way, that was an unfair trick. You knew you had lost the game, didn't you?"

"My dear Dr. Manoli," said Bell pompously, "quite the contrary would have happened. The game was as good as won."

"Sure. But by me," grinned the physician.

"Let's leave it undecided who won or lost that game. Let's concentrate on first things first!" interjected a tall, lean man with steely gray blue eyes—Perry Rhodan. He had just got to his feet and walked over to the round hatch, where he could survey the scene outside. "As far as I can make out, it looks as if the Asiatics have pulled back their forces." Stepping back from the window, he nodded pensively while he smoothed back his dark blond hair. His other hand remained in his trouser pockets all the while. Then he turned to the fourth man of the group.

"How is Khrest coming along, Dr. Haggard?"

Dr. Frank Haggard answered with the slightest hint of a smile, "From a medical point of view, Khrest's health has been completely restored. There is not a trace of his leukemia left."

"We don't have to fear for his health any more?" asked Rhodan eagerly. "He will go on living then!"

"Of course. Although I don't know for how long. The life span of the Arkonide race must be limited somehow; otherwise, they would not have set out on their search for the planet of eternal life. The alien's body seems of an extraordinary youthfulness, and his metabolism shows a surprising vitality. But judging from his looks he seems to be about fifty years of age."

"But he is much older than that," said Rhodan. "And so is Thora."

Thora, the commanding officer of the extraterrestrial race of space explorers, presented a mystery and challenge to the few humans that so far had come in contact with her. She had fascinated them by her appearance. Her light hair, more white than blond, her huge eyes of an odd golden-reddish hue and her almost yellow complexion had indicated her to be of an albinoid type. And yet she had to be called beautiful. Perry Rhodan, though, considered her beauty to be only skin deep. He was convinced that she had inside her nothing but icy cold reasoning and a steely logical mind. She seemed to lack a heart and soul. Never would she have been willing to help the human race or even to recognize them as her equals, if she had not been forced to do so by her spaceship's destruction. The space cruiser's auxiliary vessel, which in reality was an enormous space sphere almost 200 feet in diameter, was equipped with an ultralight drive, but its range extended only 500 light-years—not enough even to establish contact with the nearest base of the Arkonides.

"Thora is getting on my nerves," announced Bell as he stood up. "I know that she despises us, and she is coming to our assistance only because this way she is able to help herself. I just can't stand that."

"The Arkonides do need us, that's quite true," admitted Rhodan. He continued with emphasis, "But don't let us forget that we depend on them, too. It's a kind of symbiosis. We can't do without it if we ever want to reach our goal. And one of these goals, Reg, is the unification of mankind. The imaginary threat has had the result for the first time in human history that all the nations of the world have united, even if only to destroy us."

Haggard moved next to Rhodan and looked out of the hatch. The Arkonide space sphere reposed quite close to the *Stardust*. Inside the alien ship the generator was working to produce the mighty power field that created a protective screen around their base. The outer circular perimeter of that energy dome touched the ground at a distance of about three miles from the center. This was a fortress that could not be stormed. Even atomic bombs glanced off ineffectively from the invisible outer hull of energy.

Shiny, metallic robots hurried back and forth, anchoring the space sphere securely to the ground and busily performing many tasks. They were the only occupants of the alien space cruiser, besides Khrest and Thora, that had been saved when their moon base was annihilated. They were the lone survivors of a space expedition that had set out from a star empire whose scope could hardly be imagined by a human mind.

The Arkonides' remaining auxiliary vessel could indeed traverse a distance of 500 light-years within a few days. This was an incredible feat, measured by human standards, but unfortunately for the Arkonides, it was insufficient. Their situation could be compared to that of a shipwrecked crew stranded on an uninhabited island in the Pacific, busily building a canoe from a single tree trunk. However, the storerooms of the auxiliary vessel were bulging with spare parts and all kinds of machinery, capable of constructing whole space flotillas, if the industrial potential of Earth's economy could be harnessed to this productive effort.

This was the reason Khrest and Thora had entered into an alliance with Perry Rhodan. This offered the only way they could ever return to their home planet. With human help they could construct a ship that would reach their planets revolving around a hot, blue white sun within the star cluster M 13, more than 34,000 light-years away. This planet, Arkon, was the center of a galactic empire.

Haggard motioned toward the space sphere. "They seem to be settling down here on Earth, at least temporarily. How can they build a starship here in the desert, far removed from civilization?"

"I don't know for sure," admitted Rhodan, "but I have a pretty good idea. Don't forget that we are sitting here underneath an energy dome about six miles across. That's quite some area. I can well imagine that huge industrial facilities could be erected here. Don't you agree, Doc?"

"You mean an industrial plant for spacecraft construction?" wondered Haggard aloud. "You mean to say that . . ."

"I only suggested such a possibility," replied Rhodan softly. "I am not too well informed about Khrest's plans but I am convinced that he will need our technical assistance with them. We'll see shortly what he intends to do."

Reginald Bell, too, had got to his feet in the meantime. He yawned.

"I must confess that I'm worried about this cease fire. As long as the Chinese were busy shooting at us, they were not up to any other mischief."

Suddenly Rhodan's brow was deeply furrowed. "Any other mischief? My dear friend, this brings up an unpleasant thought. Could they use this lull to attack us in some other manner we aren't aware of yet?"

Bell turned pale. "I didn't mean it that way . . ."

"But wouldn't it be quite plausible for them to look for some other method to remove this cancer from their body? After all, that is what we are in their eyes, nothing but a cancerous growth threatening their survival. Unfortunately, we cannot observe from here whatever is going on outside. We have no friends—"

"How about Captain Klein from the intelligence agency!" Bell interrupted. "Don't you remember what he did, together with his colleagues from the Eastern Bloc, Lt. Kosnow and Lt. Li Tschai-tung from the Asiatic Secret Service? How they acted quite unmistakably in our interest when they were supposed to annihilate us! I am absolutely convinced that they would warn us if they knew of some danger."

"Yes indeed—Captain Klein." Rhodan nodded in agreement. "He is on good terms with the main command center in Greenland. He is working directly under Allan D. Mercant, and if he knew anything that would threaten us here, he would not hesitate to inform us about it."

Rhodan peered once more through the window hatch. He trembled slightly. A shadow flitted across his face, but he did not seem to be displeased by what he saw. He was, on the contrary, somehow embarrassed by it. But he quickly regained his composure.

He turned to the three men. "Thora wants to talk to me." He walked over to the door of the command center.

Now Bell in turn looked out of the hatch. Over there, next to the gigantic space sphere, stood a beautiful figure, tall and slender. Her bright hair could hardly be distinguished from the metallic background of the spacecraft. She stood quietly, waiting, every inch the unapproachable commanding officer of the stranded space expedition. Her pride forbade her to make even the slightest welcoming gesture to the approaching Earthling.

Commander Perry Rhodan could not have explained logically what attracted him to this woman. Never before in his life had he encountered someone who was more intelligent, more aloof and more arrogant. This creature from another world, who had the appearance of a woman, was heartless; she simply could not have a heart. Nevertheless, she was most beautiful.

Yet it was not her beauty that attracted Rhodan to her; it was rather her aura of inaccessibility. At first he had thought it important to persuade her that human beings, too, were intelligent and therefore had a right to exist. But soon he had recognized that only an approach of cold logic would convince someone of Thora's type. He had to make her see that man was not only intelligent but also indispensable to her plans.

She did not make the slightest effort to come to meet him. She did not stir. She waited motionless until he stood in front of her. Only then did she address him.

"They have stopped the shooting," she remarked dryly. She avoided specifying who *they* were, noted Rhodan. She would not even call them humans or terrestrials. Crass disdain was in her voice. "Why?"

Perry looked straight into her icy eyes. She met his glance steadfastly, but then a brief flicker arose in their bottomless reddish gold depths. Just a brief moment; then once again she was in complete control of herself.

"It might be that the enlargement of our energy dome has caused them to change their plans," Rhodan replied quietly. "After all, we have increased our domain to about five times its former size. They had to withdraw their troops hastily after your initial punitive measures. Although they did continue the bombardment of our positions here for some time, they seem to have worked out some other tactics in the meantime."

"This will not do them any good either."

"You might underestimate the human race," suggested Rhodan slowly. "This is not the first time for you, though. Remember what happened the last time? You lost your ship, didn't you? Why do you want to repeat your mistake?"

"I never make a mistake, I want you to know. Not I, but the robots, were responsible for the catastrophe on the moon."

"Those robots had to obey your commands and carry out your orders," corrected Rhodan calmly. It gave him an almost painful pleasure to humiliate her. "Don't you think that the protective screen might be too large now? Its scale might decrease its stability, I'm afraid."

"Let me worry about that. In my opinion even the largest atomic bomb would detonate ineffectually on the screen's surface. You don't realize the full capacity of the Arkonide reactor. It is capable of producing enough energy to throw your planet out of its usual orbit."

Rhodan knew that she was not exaggerating.

"In any case, I am very appreciative that you have limited

yourself merely to defensive measures," he said. "I fully realize that you could easily have reduced to dust the enemy army that is surrounding us. Why don't you, by the way?"

Displeasure briefly flared in her icy features.

"Khrest is against it. He probably believes he must be grateful to you for curing him of his illness."

"Shouldn't he?"

She shook her head lightly. "You look at this problem the wrong way. We are only trying to pay off a debt when we come to your assistance here. I'll admit that in some areas you are ahead of us—in the field of medicine, perhaps. But in the field of technology . . ."

She did not bother to complete her sentence. Rhodan seized the opportunity. "You are indeed far ahead of us in the field of technology; I fully realize that. But despite this superiority, even you are powerless without our help. Even if 500 light-years represent an insurmountable distance for us now, under the present circumstances, you still cannot make any use of your knowhow to bridge this distance and return home. In order to do so, both you and Khrest are fully aware that you are forced to collaborate with us. This is the only reason, the one and only reason, that you have entered into this alliance with us. We don't need to fool each other. Let's be honest!"

She did not even smile. "Little by little you are beginning to think logically, Rhodan. Our collaboration is nothing but a matter of expediency; that is all there is to it. Once both you and we have attained our goals, we will again go our separate ways. No expression of gratitude need be exchanged, because each of us will have profited by our mutual association. That is the way I see things."

"Khrest's approach is more human, if you will pardon the expression. He has a soul."

"A soul? What is that, a soul?"

Rhodan flipped his hand in a contemptuous gesture. "Maybe sometime later I'll try to explain that to you. Right now it would be a complete waste of time. Will you tell me, now, why you asked to see me?"

His matter of fact attitude and coldness had a very sobering effect, even on Thora. Little did she know what effort he had to exert to achieve this effect of aloofness.

There was a dangerous gleam in her eyes as she answered, "Our robot detachment has stabilized the energy screen. We can await any further attacks with complete calm. How soon can you provide us with the necessary help, so that we may begin with the construction of our new spaceship?"

"As soon as mankind stops fighting me. Only then can we start to assist you with your project. Unfortunately, I can't change the fact that your cooperation must precede ours. First you help us so that we can help you in turn."

"And how long will it take for the human race to understand the foolishness of trying to fight against us?"

"Never, unfortunately, as far as I know them. Unless they are forced to do so by radical means." He smiled coldly. "We are a race of warriors still, I regret to say."

She regarded him. For an instant Rhodan seemed to perceive a sign of sympathy in her glance; but it was probably just an illusion on his part.

"So were we," she remarked, "once upon a time when we were young and immature. This attitude will pass only when the race has become mature and wise."

"And has grown old!" added Rhodan.

He was rather surprised that she nodded in agreement without growing angry at him. "You are right, unfortunately."

With these words she turned around and walked toward the space sphere.

CHAPTER TWO

AN UNOBTRUSIVE looking man sat behind the desk.

He was rather short, youngish in appearance, and he exuded an impression of almost unbelievable harmlessness.

A thin wreath of golden locks circled his bald dome. Here and there near his temples a few white hairs could be seen. His eyes regarded the world around him with a beatific expression.

For the time being, this world consisted solely of a technically perfectly arranged office, almost two miles underground, deep below the permanent ice of Greenland. This was the headquarters of the best organized secret service of the world, the Intelligence Agency. This special organization had been formed during the Cold War and was under the command of NATO. The harmless man behind the desk was the head of this organization, Allan D. Mercant, one of the most feared men of the twentieth century.

A screen lit up.

"The heads of the secret services have arrived, sir."

"Eastern Bloc and Asiatic Federation?"

"Iwan Martinowitsch Kosselow from the Eastern Bloc and Mao-tsen from the Asiatic Federation," confirmed the announcer from the communications center. "Lieutenant General Tai-tiang has just landed. He has been escorted to the electrolift already."

"Well, the whole clan is assembled then," Mercant nodded and leaned back in his seat. He waited until the screen grew dark before he smiled mildly.

Only a few short weeks ago it would have been absurd even to imagine in one's wildest dreams the events that were now taking place. The men who once had been the bitterest enemies, the highest in command of the secret service and espionage organizations, were now meeting in the Headquarters of the Western Intelligence Agency. They had a common purpose now—to destroy a common foe.

Mercant's smile grew suddenly bitter.

And what would happen in case they succeeded in their task? He knew the answer the moment he thought of the question. There was a strange fire in his eyes as he bent forward slightly to push a button.

Another screen lit up. On it the head of a pretty girl became visible. "Mr. Mercant?"

"Please see to it that the three men who have been accommodated in the transfer hotel are called to the conference too. Their names are Captain Klein, Lieutenant Li

Tschai-tung and Lieutenant Kosnow. Let them wait in the outer office until I call for them. Is that clear?"

"Perfectly, sir," The pretty girl nodded, and her picture disappeared from the screen. Mercant stared at the empty screen for another second before he rose from his seat.

This conference room had been chosen other than the one where the plans for the moon expedition had been discussed and decided. This time Mercant had placed the utmost importance on complete secrecy. There was no trace of any hidden microphone or other electronic snooping device; there were no secretly running tape recorders or noiselessly working cameras. The room was small, with only one door and not even an air conditioning system. There was only one vacuum pump that sucked out the used-up air, which was constantly replenished by bottles of compressed air standing in a corner of the room. Admittedly, this was a rather primitive arrangement, but it was proof against any unwelcome listeners.

And Mercant knew only too well why he did not want to risk any unwelcome listeners.

Three men were sitting at the table when Mercant entered the room. They interrupted their conversation, which they had carried on in Russian, and rose.

Mercant smiled innocuously. "It's a pleasure to be able to welcome you here, gentlemen. We owe this happy occasion to our common foe. Thanks to him, we are sitting here united around the conference table. Too bad that one day soon we will finish off this enemy, don't you agree?"

Lieutenant General Tai-tiang, commander in chief of the encircling troops, seemed to be nonplussed. It was evident that he did not know how to interpret this startling remark.

Iwan Martinowitsch Kosselow, Chief of Defense of the Eastern Bloc, reacted quite differently, however. He broke out a wide grin, slapped his ruddy, fleshy cheek and roared loudly, "I am not so sure that your President would be pleased to hear that kind of talk. But our conversation won't go beyond these walls, I hope."

Mao-tsen, chief of the Asiatic Federation defense department, smiled enigmatically. This was all the comment he cared to make.

Mercant shook hands with his three guests and asked them to be seated again. Suddenly his face turned serious, as if someone had wiped away his friendly smile.

"Rest assured, my dear colleague," he said to Kosselow, "there isn't another human being on this Earth who can hear whatever we discuss in this room. We are hermetically sealed off from the outside world. The door has been electronically locked, and in case I should suddenly suffer a heart attack, your own organizations would have to go on without your leadership, for nobody would come to let you out of here. Maybe in a year or two, people would start wondering how long this session was taking. But by then it would be too late for you anyhow."

"You have a rather odd sense of humor," observed Mao with a smile, although his yellow complexion had become a trifle darker momentarily. "But let's come to the point! Let's listen to our friend's report now!"

Lieutenant General Tai-tiang was apparently still pondering the meaning of Mercant's words, for he was startled when he was addressed by Mao-tsen. But he quickly regained his composure. His voice sounded more and more confident as he proceeded with his account.

"We followed the advice of our experts and kept aiming our missiles so that they hit Rhodan's energy screen head on, all the time at the same spot. A certain weakening could be observed, but this success was only of a very short duration. Then, just a few days ago, Rhodan enlarged his domain. Until then the diameter of the energy dome had been roughly three miles. Now it has grown to six miles. The enemy's territory covers an area of almost thirty square miles right in the middle of the realm of the Asiatic Federation. This is an intolerable situation."

"It is just as intolerable for the other parties concerned," confirmed Mercant. "What countermeasures did you take?"

"We withdrew our troops in time, after we had been warned by Rhodan. Then we renewed our fire from our shortened lines. Although our fire power had been strengthened considerably in the meantime, now the screen no longer showed any weak spots. Apparently this is due to the incredible capacity of the Arkonides' generators, which were transported inside the space sphere coming from the moon. I must admit that in the face of such strength we are simply helpless. We had to cease our bombardment a few days later. We ran out of ammunition. Since then calm reigns around the enemy's base. But inside the energy bell we have observed a great deal of activity. They seem to be erecting several smaller buildings. Their purpose is unknown to us at this point. There are plenty of robots but only four human beings and the two Arkonides. The base is completely sealed off from the outside world. As far as we know, no one has entered or left it."

Mercant nodded quietly. "Nobody except our agents Klein, Kosnow and Li."

"Unfortunately, their mission was unsuccessful," boomed Kosselow's mighty voice. "Isn't it time to repeat this experiment?"

"This is exactly why I have invited you to come here," said Mercant. "But first I would like to discuss our position with you. We must be sure where we are. General Tai, do you think it is absolutely impossible to seize the enemy's stronghold, attacking it from the outside? Are you convinced that there aren't any bombs capable of penetrating this energy screen?"

Tai-tiang nodded in silent agreement. Mercant looked at the chief of the Asiatic defense organization.

"Well, Mao, what is your opinion? Can you come up with any suggestions?"

The Chinese had regained his natural color in the meantime. His smile was still as enigmatic as before, however.

"Our agents were unable to accomplish their task. Even if they came as close to their target as was necessary. Our agent Lieutenant Li, nevertheless, does not know anything we did not already know before. I am sorry, but I am at my wits' end."

Mercant's glance kept wandering on until it rested on the Russian Kosselow.

"Kosselow?"

"I could simply repeat what our Chinese colleague just said. But that would be too easy a way out. Frankly, I have been thinking a great deal these past few days how we could save this precarious situation, how we could turn it to our own advantage. As usual, there is always something good to be found even in the most hopeless appearing situations. You, Mr. Mercant, hinted at such a possibility at the beginning of this meeting. Isn't it true that Rhodan has accomplished something that is to our mutual advantage —we are peacefully assembled here to discuss matters of common concern to us? Necessity brought us together, isn't it so? The former opponents are the friends of today."

"Well, well!" muttered Lieutenant General Tai-tiang, and cleared his throat. As he was about to continue a glance from Mao-tsen made him change his mind. He fell silent.

"Yes, indeed, friends!" repeated Kosselow seriously. "And why is that so? How has this come about? Only because we are all afraid of Rhodan! We know that we are powerless to fight against his superior technical machines. We realize only too clearly that he could destroy us, if he so desired. Sometimes it worries me that he does not do so."

"What a macabre comment," smiled Mercant, with his usual mild expression. "But right to the point. You have assessed our situation correctly. Go on, Kosselow! I am anxious to hear what conclusions you have drawn from your observations."

"I'd rather not tell you, at this point. But as regards other matters, I want to be completely frank with you. According to General Tai we will never succeed in destroying Rhodan's base from the outside. If that is the case, why don't we then attack from the inside?"

"Very interesting, indeed. And how would you do that?"

"As usual, people think last of the most obvious solution. Just take your case, Mr. Mercant. Where do you feel safest? Right here, deep down below the ground! Whoever wanted to annihilate you and your headquarters would have to attack you from below. What is the difference between Rhodan's energy bell, which shields him from any attack coming from the air, and this rocky cover, stretching above us for thousands of feet? If you want to get at him, you too must attack him from below, from underneath the ground on which his base stands."

For a while there was silence in the room. Only the rhythmic breathing of the men could be heard. Kosselow was leaning back in his chair, waiting to see the effect his words had on the others.

Mercant spoke up first. "Well, this makes the second point on which we seem to agree, Kosselow. We had arrived at the same conclusion as far as politics were concerned, even if we did not express this in words. And now we find ourselves in agreement as regards strategy. You have guessed at my plans accurately. Will you permit me to include now in our discussion the three men who know the base better than any one of us?"

Without waiting for their reply, Mercant pushed a button directly in front of him. The door opened a few seconds later. Somebody peered into the room, Mercant motioned to him briefly, and the person disappeared.

Then Captain Albrecht Klein, Lieutenant Kosnow and Lieutenant Li Tschai-tung entered the conference room. The door quickly closed behind them.

Mercant pointed to three empty seats. "No need to introduce you to each other, since you all are well acquainted. But in a few minutes you will meet someone whom none of you have known of so far. Especially you, Kosselow, will be amazed to learn how much our views coincide. Captain Klein, you have already explained to us the reasons why you failed in your attempt to wipe out the *Stardust* base and its crew with an attack using deadly bacteria. May I assume that you will approve of another plan of annihilation of the enemy? No, this time no bacteria!"

The door opened again. A man entered, dressed in the uniform of a colonel. He saluted stiffly; then he remained standing and waited until Mercant rose to introduce him.

"Gentlemen, may I present to you Colonel Donald Cretcher of the IIA. Colonel Cretcher is an expert in underground construction and was mainly responsible for building the subterranean installations of these headquarters."

The chiefs of defense greeted the newcomer uneasily. General Tai-tiang, in particular, could hardly conceal his feelings of distrust. Kosselow was the only one present who had listened attentively when Cretcher's special field of interest had been mentioned.

Mercant began to speak. "Kosselow has already hinted at the solution, that we must attack Rhodan from underneath his base. The energy screen is effective in the surrounding atmosphere, but it does not reach below the surface of the Earth. So far, of course, we have no conclusive evidence how far the underground range of the energy dome may extend. But I sincerely do not believe that it could work in any other medium except the air. If, therefore, we should succeed in drilling a shaft through the underground rocks deep enough and far enough so that it will end exactly below the base, we could finish off this whole unholy mess by detonating an atomic bomb at that spot. That, very briefly, is my plan. I have asked you to gather here to discuss the execution of this new strategy, for all the big powers must be willing to cooperate. First and foremost, the Asiatic Federation, since we will be operating inside their territory."

While Klein was listening to Mercant's words, thoughts were racing feverishly through his brain. Kosnow and Li, too, seemed to be absorbed in their thoughts. These three had been given the task, by each of their respective government agencies, of wiping out the *Stardust*. The three had met and joined forces when they realized they could not accomplish their job going their separate ways. But Klein had managed to penetrate the energy dome once before, and his second encounter with Rhodan had convinced him more than ever that the former commander of the first moon landing expedition was motivated by only the highest and noblest intentions for the good of all mankind. Klein in turn then had been able to persuade his two colleagues of Rhodan's integrity. Not a single soul on earth could know of this "high treason"!

Or could they have been mistaken? Did someone know?

Allan D. Mercant looked at Klein. There was a strange glimmer in his eyes, which was quickly replaced by his usual expression of gentle understanding.

"In case this plan should succeed, it would also mean the end of a fear that has made friends of former enemies. I know that there are people who fear this, for they prefer this to the constant horror of impending atomic war, with its threat of total destruction of life as we know it on Earth. I even know some of these people, and perhaps I share their opinion. But it is our duty, I must emphasize, to eliminate Perry Rhodan. He must be rendered harmless, for he represents a danger that we cannot handle, and thus he endangers our very existence. Have I made myself sufficiently clear, Captain Klein?"

Seven pairs of eyes were directed toward the secret agent, who seemed to feel the ground tremble under his feet. Was it possible that Mercant had found out something?

"I don't understand you, Mr. Mercant."

Mercant maintained his kindly smile. "You do understand me very well, Klein. Very well indeed. And please, don't you believe for a single moment that I can overlook punishable deeds, just because they were committed with the most honorable intentions. You will be requested to carry out a task whereby you can demonstrate to our satisfaction that complying with duty is more important to you than following the dictates of your own personal feelings. The same thing, by the way, also applies to Kosnow and Li."

Kosselow stormed angrily, "I'd stake my reputation on our man!"

"I wouldn't be that careless with my reputation!" warned Mercant calmly.

"You have no proof for your allegations!"

"That might be true. But I have an excellent nose for such things—I have an unerring instinct."

This was no exaggeration. Klein knew how much Mercant was feared in this respect by the people around him. Mercant never had to use a lie detector during cross examinations. He was always positive whether someone told the truth or not. Some of his agents were even sure that Mercant could read their minds.

Mao-tsen joined the conversation. "We have met here to work out the best way to fight against Perry Rhodan but not to accuse our best agents. Whatever you plan to do with your own man is your own affair. But will you kindly leave our agent, Lieutenant Li, alone. I have full confidence in him, regardless of what you might say. May I suggest now that we start discussing the details of our plan."

"You are right—this is why we are assembled here," said Mercant, and pulled a map out of a briefcase. He placed the map on the table in front of him, the men were all soon bent over it while they listened intently.

"This is the exact position of Rhodan's base in the Gobi Desert. This circle represents the area covered by the energy dome. As you can see, this comprises even part of the lake. We might have a chance to get inside the bell here by using some diving equipment. We could simply dive and swim underneath the outside perimeter of the energy screen into that part of the lake which lies inside the base. But what good would it do to get a few men over to their side? We all know the kinds of weapons Rhodan has, which would render our men ineffective at once. No, we are forced to proceed in a radical manner if we want to succeed. I have discussed this with Colonel Cretcher, and perhaps he can explain directly to you how he envisions carrying out the best strategy."

The colonel nodded briefly. He pulled the map over to his side a little more and placed his hand on a spot north of the circle.

"Right about here, more than a mile from the outer perimeter of the energy dome, there are a few low hills. While they ascend quite gradually from south to north, their walls are rather steep on the northern side. This slope will be the ideal point where we can begin to drive a shaft into the rocky ground, since neither of the space rockets can overlook what is going on here on the other side. We would have to build this shaft toward the center of Rhodan's base for a distance of about four miles to reach a spot directly underneath his installations. These excavations must take place at a depth of at least 1,500 feet, to minimize the danger of detection by their listening devices. I admit that this is a rather bold plan, but it is also absolutely safe and sound!"

Kosselow and Mao-tsen looked at each other. Their eyes bespoke amazement and approval at the same time. Lieutenant General Tai-tiang pointed with his index finger to the hills on the map and nodded to confirm Cretcher's statement.

"I know these hills very well. This is the exact place of our gun emplacements. By the way, Colonel Cretcher, how did you find out so much about this spot?"

The chief of the IIA smiled mysteriously.

"But my dear general! We naturally have a few confidential agents serving in your army. Besides, don't forget that Western officers were officially permitted to inspect the area and your military installations there. As you see, things have a quite natural explanation."

"Yes, of course. Excuse me. Well, you mean to say then that the northern hill will be the most favorable starting point for this action?"

"Absolutely. And as soon as we are sitting right smack below the spaceships we will detonate an H bomb. Guess what will remain of Rhodan and his friends from out of space?"

"Not too much," admitted Kosselow, and scratched his head pensively. "But still, I can't imagine that the Arkonides would not figure out such a possibility themselves. I am sure that they will safeguard themselves against any such eventuality."

"We have thought of this too," assured Mercant. "It would be wrong, of course, if we should remain quiet and inactive now. On the contrary, General Tai-tiang will have to resume his nonstop barrage as soon as the digging commences. Maybe not as intense as before but still strong enough to keep Rhodan and his associates busy. And don't forget that the detonation of the missiles will drown out the noises that will be inevitable when we explode our underground charges while digging the tunnel. In addition to that, it is quite impossible that Rhodan should learn of our enterprise, since his base is hermetically sealed off from the outside world. This extends even to any radio communication. We have placed strong jamming stations around the base that prevent reception of outside signals. Even if someone should try it, there is no way of warning Perry Rhodan of our plans."

The same mild glimmer as before became visible in Mercant's eyes as they made a brief round from Klein and Kosnow and finally to Li.

Colonel Cretcher pointed to the map. "We will organize an international squad. Each nation will contribute its best men. Together we will finally succeed in removing this common foe of mankind for good."

"He is an American, after all," muttered the Chinese Maotsen under his breath.

"He *was* an American!" corrected Mercant sharply. "You must be aware that he was drummed out of the air force and stripped of his rank. But this doesn't matter any longer. We are facing an invasion from outer space. We must repulse this attack, come what may, for if we don't succeed we will soon cease to be masters of this planet."

There was a short pause.

Lieutenant Kosnow, agent of the Eastern Bloc, interrupted the silence. "What·particular task will we have to carry out?"

Mercant smiled. "I was waiting for this question. It is obvious that any international contingent has its weak spots. Rhodan has some friends among us, there is no doubt about it. Perhaps some of his friends will even be working with the detonation crew, although there won't be much they can do to help him there. But I want to make sure that the men of this squad will be under constant surveillance. Since we cannot do this alone, I thought it would be advisable to employ here a team of agents whose sole duty would be to guard the security of this enterprise. I believe I made myself sufficiently clear, didn't I?"

Klein was observing Mercant while he spoke to the assembly. There was no hint in Mercant's eyes of what was going on behind his forehead. And yet it seemed to Klein that he could sense a challenging irony hidden in the IIA Chief's words.

Lieutenant General Tai-tiang rapped his knuckles lightly on the map. "As soon as new supplies of ammunition reach my positions in these hills, I'll be ready to start shooting again. How long, do you estimate, will it take to finish building the shaft?"

Colonel Cretcher shrugged his shoulders.

"It will take a few days to get that detonation crew together. The job itself might last about two weeks, provided we have the most modern machines at our disposal. It will also depend, naturally, on the ground formations. In case we find mainly rock . . ."

"Quite likely at this depth!"

"Well, let's say about three weeks. Perhaps in another

month there will be a gaping crater in the Gobi Desert, and Perry Rhodan and the Arkonides will become a soon forgotten legend."

"Which nevertheless brought us a short period of peace among the nations of the world!" concluded Kosselow with emphasis.

Later, when Allan D. Mercant was again sitting all alone in his office and letting the events of the past hours pass review in his mind's eye, Kosselow's last remark stood out in particular. Mercant knew that Iwan Martinowitsch Kosselow must have his doubts about this affair—the same way he did. Only Mao-tsen, Chief of the Secret Service of the Asiatic Federation was absolutely sure of himself and totally uncompromising in his views. As far as the Chinese was concerned, Rhodan was the arch enemy who must be destroyed. Mao did not waste any thoughts about what would come afterward. But Kosselow did, and so did Mercant.

Klein, too, must be one of those persons who think very intensely. Perhaps this was the reason Mercant was capable of receiving some of his strong brain waves, which he could interpret in some vague manner.

Mercant smiled. He knew that his people called him a magician when he told them what they were thinking about. He was not a mind reader or a telepath, but he was still capable of sensing other people's emotions. There were so many areas of the brain that lay fallow, unused, that perhaps a small stimulus was sufficient to awaken some of them. This is what must have happened to him. If he worked at it, he must surely improve this so far limited faculty of mind reading.

Perhaps he was a mutant. Mercant contemplated his slender fingers, then shook his head. No, he was not a mutant in the true sense of the word. Yet he possessed some extraordinary talents that enabled him to distinguish whether someone was speaking the truth.

And thus he knew with absolute certainty that at today's conference of eight participants, exactly half sympathized at least partially with Perry Rhodan.

He almost forgot the fifth person, who was forced to follow unconditionally his government's orders but who was already hesitating deep inside, in his heart, and who had seriously begun to ponder Rhodan's true aims.

Namely, himself.

CHAPTER THREE

NOT A SINGLE shot had been fired during the past five days.

The four men of the *Stardust I* sensed that something important and decisive was in the offing, but they could not divine what it was. Reginald Bell was highly irritated and was always pacing the corridors of the ship like a captured beast of prey, except when he preferred to roam around the outside of the aliens' space sphere and watch the robots busy working at their tasks. Every day he swam in the part of the lake that was protected by the dome of the energy screen. The air inside the dome had become oppressive and very humid. Frequently he extended his excursions into the desert. He would walk there for hours and occasionally dared to advance as far as the invisible wall that separated them all from the outside world.

Not a human being was in sight. They seemed to be all alone on this planet. The troops that had formerly surrounded the spaceship's base had withdrawn so far to the rear that they could be recognized only now and then as tiny dots. Not a trace was to be seen of any of the guns and tanks.

There was something in the air.

Even Rhodan could feel it. Spurned on by an inner restlessness, he decided on the fifth day to leave *Stardust I* and walk over to the space sphere. He had seen very little of Khrest these last days, for the Arkonide scientist was closely obeying the instructions of his physician, Dr. Haggard, who had brought about his recovery from leukemia. Most of the time, the alien was resting in a state of artificial sleep that afforded his blood a better chance of regeneration.

One of the robots was blocking the entrance to the space-sphere.

Perry waited for a few minutes, but when he was convinced that the metallic guard would not move from his spot he approached him and tried to push him aside—unsuccessfully, of course.

From high above the entrance rang out Thora's voice: "You should be more cautious, Rhodan. Luckily for you that we could save only our work robots. All our soldier robots but one perished during the attack on our moon base. And this soldier robot is still being repaired. You would not have liked how he would have dealt with an intruder. What do you want here?"

"I must talk to Khrest."

"Why?"

"For various reasons. Most important, that they are preparing to attack us again."

"So what! Do you still have any doubt that we are able to defend ourselves?"

"That is not the point. You know that we need the people of this world to carry out our plans. If you should annihilate the human race while warding off their assault, you will never see again your home planet, Arkon."

With this reply Rhodan touched a sore spot in Thora's character. She was burning inside to "teach a lesson to these rebellious primitives." But she was frustrated by Khrest, as well as Rhodan. This hurt the pride that she felt as female commander of the Arkonide scientific expedition. But on the other hand, she realized that both these men were right. After all, it was impossible to create the necessary installations for spaceship construction exclusively with the help of their worker robots.

She uttered a command in a strange language. Awkwardly, the robot stomped aside to let Rhodan pass. Rhodan climbed up the few steps to the open hatch, where Thora welcomed him with an icy stare.

"Khrest is in need of rest."

"I am fully aware of that," answered Perry, unperturbed

by her hostility. "But I have Dr. Haggard's permission to talk to him now."

"Well, Haggard authorized you to do so?" she replied with disdain. "You seem to have forgotten to obtain the consent from the proper authorities. How about asking *my* permission?"

"That is unnecessary in this case," answered Perry Rhodan, and pushed gently past her. Without looking back at her, he walked on to the antigrav lift and floated upward.

Khrest was awake. He was resting on a wide couch in the roomy cabin and was watching an abstract color program on the picture screen. When Rhodan entered, he switched off the set and sat up.

"Hello, Perry. Glad to see you. Nice that you find a little time to visit me again."

"The pleasure is all mine. How are you feeling? According to Haggard you seem to undergo a period of rejuvenation."

"Yes, indeed. I feel born again. This man has worked miracles with me."

"He is our most outstanding physician," agreed Rhodan.

Khrest, too, had very light, almost white hair and reddish eyes. His unusually high skull caused his forehead to extend to more than half the size of his whole head. All other characteristics that distinguished the alien from the human race were of an organic nature. Instead of a rib cage enclosing and protecting the vital organs of heart and lungs, Khrest had a solid, bony thorax. This certainly afforded better protection against injury but would make it more difficult to gain access in case of a needed operation.

Compared with human beings, Khrest was a genius. His photographic memory was similar to the workings of an electronic brain. He was a living computer of the highest capacity.

"Unfortunately, we do not have anyone to compare to Dr. Haggard," continued Khrest. "Maybe this is the reason our race fell ill. We are in possession of the means for prolonging life, and this made us careless. We began to degenerate, for our boundless conceit did not permit us to mix with other races. We are a highly inbred race—all of us are somehow related."

"I have mentioned already that your people are in need of new blood."

"How do you imagine that to come about practically?" asked Khrest, smiling feebly. "I admit that your physical and mental capacities are young and strong. Combined with our superior knowledge, this might result in a race of giant intellects—of course, only from a theoretical point of view, to begin with, for it would take many generations for the results of such a fantastic experiment to become evident. No, I believe that we are past any help; we have waited too long. And besides, can you really seriously imagine that Thora would ever consider mingling her blood with that of a human being who is only a primitive in her eyes?"

"Definitely not," Rhodan shook his head.

Khrest pushed a button. The concave wall next to his bed slid aside, and an oval shaped window appeared. Rhodan noticed that they were about 120 feet above the ground. A magnificent view of the surrounding desert spread out in front of them. The sun was high in the sky behind the ship. Far to the north there was a chain of low lying hills.

"This landscape reminds me in some ways of my own home planet, at least the way it must have looked a long time ago," said Khrest softly. "But then we became the focal point of a galactic empire, and we could no longer permit ourselves the luxury of a genuinely natural envirnoment."

"I would like to be able to visit Arkon someday, Khrest."

The white haired scientist smiled indulgently. "You might be disappointed, Perry. Our world, as big as your own, is nothing but one huge city. One immense, hollowed out honeycomb. Nevertheless, someday you will see Arkon."

Perry leaned forward, surprised. "I? Able to see Arkon? How?"

Khrest lay down again. He looked up at the low ceiling of the cabin; then he fixed his glance on Rhodan. "Yes, you will visit Arkon, Perry Rhodan. Perhaps I did not make myself clear when I spoke of regenerating our own blood. There can never be a mingling of our races, for yours would be the loser in this process. But there is a possibility that once mankind is united—but definitely not before that point

—the human race, guided by the Arkonides, might take over the heritage of the galactic empire. What do you think of such a dream for the future?"

Rhodan breathed deeply. "Too fantastic a dream to be considered seriously, Khrest. You are masters of a galaxy wide realm, and you would never abdicate your power voluntarily. On the other hand, man is too immature yet even to dare dream of such an empire."

"I am afraid that you, too, underestimate man's potential," Khrest said. "I had many an occasion to discuss these matters with Dr. Haggard. He shares my view in this respect."

"Even if I should believe in man's dormant capabilities, I could not deceive myself that the Arkonides would be capable of such a display of unselfishness."

"Don't judge us by Thora!" admonished Khrest gently. "She is the commanding officer of an expedition and has been specially trained for this task. Her sharp and logical mind is the result of intensive indoctrination."

"What do you mean by that?"

"Indoctrination is a hypnotic method of teaching that activates the parts of the brain that lie fallow, while the parts that are already functioning become intensified."

"Training by hypnosis then, isn't it?"

"Yes, if you prefer to call it that. With this method you can transform a primitive creature into an intelligent being, provided, of course, that it has a brain to begin with. I intend to use this approach to transmit some of our own knowledge to you."

Rhodan stepped back instinctively. "What? You want to . . . ?" he was gasping for air. "Why?"

Khrest was still smiling. "You are so full of distrust, my friend. You assume I could not do anything unselfish. You are right to some extent. I am thinking far ahead, of times to come. With bold strokes I am painting a picture of the future, but this is not solely the future of the Arkonides. They will no longer be alone. Two related races will rule the galaxy, the Arkonides together with the Terrans. Please, Perry, note the expression 'Terrans.' You are probably aware of the tremendous difference between a human being and a Terran. You, Perry, went out into space, and this automatically made you a Terran. Everybody changes into a

Terran, once he experiences the feeling of being able to close his hands around the globe. The others, though, especially those who are attacking us, are nothing but human beings who are completely unaware that their home planet, Earth, represents only a starting base for the future. All intelligent life has originated from the ocean, for this is where the archetypical cell was born. But the ocean belongs to the same category of environment as the universe. Thus, man returns to his original home when he moves out into space. And someday in the future, once the Terrans and the Arkonides have solidified their star realm, Earth will have become nothing but a legend. This world will be lost amidst the millions of tiny specks of light in the infinity of a borderless ocean."

Khrest fell silent for a few minutes. This gave Rhodan the opportunity to absorb this colossal vision of the future.

Then Khrest continued, "In a few centuries the Arkonides will no longer be able to hold together their empire. Already now and then some planets are trying to regain their independence. Needless to say, this independence would not do them much good, since they would only use it to tear each other to pieces. Therefore, to maintain general peace within the galaxy, we must make sure that a strong hand holds the reins. Unfortunately, though, the Arkonides become increasingly incapable of fulfilling this task. But rather than permitting the collapse of this cosmic empire and witnessing its conquest by some stronger and perhaps more cruel ruler, we prefer to share our power with an ally who owes his position of strength to us. We want friends that feel obligated and grateful to us for the help we gave them. We have never before encountered a race who would be more suitable for this purpose than your own, the inhabitants of the planet Earth near the edge of the galaxy. Do you understand, now, that I am acting selfishly by making you strong?"

Perry Rhodan nodded slowly in agreement. He understood.

"These are the reasons that decided me to entrust you to our indoctrinator, even if this goes against Thora's wishes. But I feel the need to have two human beings on my side. Will you please tell me the name of your best friend. I want him to obtain the same schooling via the indoctrinator that you will get. Am I wrong in assuming that you will suggest Reginald Bell's name to me?"

Rhodan nodded assent. "What does this hypnotic schooling process entail?"

"Don't worry that we will waste any time," smiled the Arkonide scientist. "If we can start right away, today, then already by tomorrow you and your friend Bell will possess more knowledge than is shared by all the world collectively. In addition to that, certain areas of your brain will become activated that would remain dormant for many thousands of years if you let events follow their natural course of normal development or mutationally induced progress. As I have already mentioned, to a certain extent you will receive some telepathic powers; that much I know for sure. But I cannot predict what other dormant characteristics will be awakened. Quite possibly they will become activated, although not fully developed."

"That sounds really incredible."

"You will comprehend this process better once you share our knowledge. We have brought such an indoctrinator with us in order to educate less intelligent races. This enables those whom we have treated to become mental giants who can then transmit to their own race advanced ideas that will lead them along the path of progress. It is nothing but an artificial acceleration of a process that would take too long under normal circumstances. As far as you are concerned, I am proceeding much more radically. There will be no intermediate steps. I will have you jump across the gap of many millennia. You will turn into a type of man that will perhaps become the norm in another 10,000 years, when the galactic empire will be firmly entrenched on the basis the Arkonides have built before."

Again Khrest was silent, leaving Rhodan time to ponder these new facts.

Now Perry began to comprehend the apparently magnanimous attitude of the alien scientist. By helping man, he served foremost his own interest and that of his own race.

Perry pondered this thought. A logical solution for this particular situation.

"I am willing to go along with your plans," he said

calmly, despite his inner excitement. "But what will Thora have to say to this?"

Khrest shrugged. "She will have to come to terms with the idea. After all, I am the scientific leader of this expedition and must make the decisions."

"But she is the commander!" objected Rhodan.

"True enough. That means that she is responsible for the spaceship and the flight but not for scientific measures. These are solely my responsibility. You can rest assured that I know exactly what I am doing."

Rhodan did not doubt this for an instant.

Two hours later Khrest took Rhodan and Bell to a part of the space sphere that had been inaccessible to them up to this point. In the midst of complicated machinery connected by an apparent confusion of cables, were two isolated chairs with electronic helmets. These helmets were provided with several metal clamps that led into the machines. Somewhere an ominous hum could be heard, and an array of lights blinked constantly on and off.

The white haired scientist pointed to the two chairs. "The indoctrinator. Have a seat, please. You will lose consciousness and will not be aware of what is going on around you. The installation functions automatically. You see here a scale where I will set the exact amount of knowledge to be transferred to you. As you have probably noticed already, I have selected the highest possible degree for both of you. This will bring you up to the mental level of the Arkonides. As far as your inborn character is concerned, it will remain unchanged."

Reginald Bell regarded the helmets with obvious distrust. "This reminds me too much of the hot seats in Sing-Sing."

"What do you mean by Sing-Sing?" inquired Khrest.

"That is an institution for locking up criminals," Rhodan enlightened him sarcastically. "Reg is afraid to share their fate of getting electrocuted on these seats, which resemble electric chairs where criminals are executed for their crimes against society."

"Just sit down. You won't feel a thing," Khrest reassured the hesitant Bell.

Rhodan felt a light prickling sensation on his skin after Khrest had attached the clamps to the machinery. The hum grew stronger. Khrest placed his hand on a yellow lever and looked at them.

"You will fall asleep in a few seconds and wake up again at once. At least, this is the way it will seem to you. In reality, twenty-four hours will have passed by then. Let's hope though that nothing will happen in the meantime, for an interruption might endanger the result of this lightning quick training. If necessary, Haggard or Manoli will have to decide what needs to be done. All right then, we are ready . . ."

"Stop!" shouted an angry voice from the opened door. Thora was standing there, her gold red eyes ablaze with fury and hatred, her fists clenched in anger.

"I forbid you to proceed with this indoctrination, Khrest! Nothing can take place on this vessel without my previous consent! The human race is not fit to be advanced to a higher level of knowledge. They are a martial race, too fond of war. They would constitute a threat to us if they were suddenly endowed with superior intelligence."

Khrest kept his hand on the lever, unmoving. "You are mistaken, Thora. They will help us to save our empire. I have tried to explain to you the reasons for this action, but you simply refuse to understand. I am sorry about that. We need Perry Rhodan and the human race if we don't wish to perish. Our elite is dying out—"

"We won't die out if we find the planet of eternal life."

Khrest smiled gently. "Thora, have you ever considered that the old story of the planet of eternal life might have been meant symbolically? Might it not be in a figurative sense that this world is the planet of eternal life that we are seeking? But enough of this now," he added in a firmer tone. "Don't disturb me here. I must finish this work. We will talk more about it later."

Thora's voice grew more threatening. "If you insist on proceeding with this indoctrination I will use the gravitractor and cause this planet to fall into the sun!"

Khrest turned pale. "You wouldn't dare, Thora! It would be a crime against our basic laws. Wait for me in my cabin! We will discuss the whole matter again, while the indoctrinator is doing its work here."

Before Thora had a chance to reply, Khrest pushed the lever forward.

The humming became unbearable. Perry Rhodan felt his blood pounding in his throbbing temples. He could hear Bell's groaning next to him. Gradually everything turned dark in front of his eyes, and he felt himself sinking down into a bottomless pit.

A few seconds later he was completely unconscious. . . .

CHAPTER FOUR

STRANGE EVENTS took place during the week long suspension of open hostilities.

Lively activity unfolded in the hills to the north of the Gobi Desert base. Some troops were withdrawn, and others arrived. Machines and tractors were brought in from the north and parked in specially prepared depressions in the ground. They were soon hidden by camouflage nets. An army of experts began their work. Surveyors determined the location of the entrance to the shaft. Lieutenant General Tai-tiang supplied his guns with ammunition. Everyone awaited the green signal to go ahead.

In the meantime, across the hills to the south, inside the Arkonide space sphere, time was racing by for Perry Rhodan and Reginald Bell and leaving its trace on their brains in the form of concentrated knowledge. Dormant cells were awakened to sudden life and began to grow.

Khrest had used force to prevent Thora from carrying out her threat to annihilate mankind. She finally agreed to await the result of the experiment. Somehow, Khrest thought, her threat had not been meant seriously, when she had declared her intention to let the Earth fall into the sun.

Four additional events took place in various parts of the world, events that accelerated the development that began to take shape. These events seemed to occur independently of each other, but actually they were linked quite closely. They had a common origin, which dated back more than a quarter of a century.

At that time there had been visible for the first time in human history a mushroom cloud whose shape was destined to become the symbol of a new era.

It had been a crazy idea right from the beginning. Fred Hangler had known this from the very first moment. But the decision was not up to him. This was the boss's job. Trying to rob the Central Bank of Brisbane, in the middle of the day! It simply could not work!

Everything had been planned to the smallest detail. Outside in front of the entrance, the black limousine was waiting. The boss was sitting in the back seat, cradling a machine gun on his knees. The car door was slightly ajar. Next to the driver stood Jules Arnold, one hand hidden in his trouser pocket. He kept continuous watch on the road ahead, especially the traffic cop on the next corner. The policeman had no idea what was brewing just a block away. He stood under a big umbrella, waving his arms as if he were conducting an orchestra, rather than regulating the traffic in Brisbane, on the east coast of Australia.

Fred had been given the most difficult job to do. He was to enter the bank and force the two tellers to hand over the money reposing inside the vault safes. It would not occur to anybody that anything of the sort could take place just before lunchtime; they would be taken completely by surprise. Furthermore, it was general knowledge that around this time of the day all the police forces were feverishly waiting for their well deserved *siesta,* and thus their vigilance was at low ebb.

Fred Hangler knew that everything had to go very fast. It was impossible to avoid an alarm's being given. Hangler was not in the least interested in killing an employee of the bank. He was perhaps willing to sacrifice a few years of his life behind bars but not to make the supreme sacrifice and finish his life at the end of a rope.

As soon as he had the money, he would run to the car waiting outside. Just a short, fast trip and they would disappear in Jeremy's garage. A couple of minutes later the car would have another color and new license plates. The traffic cop at the corner would make his sworn statements quite in vain. The vehicle he had seen drive off at a crazy speed would have disappeared without a trace.

The boss had thought of everything. He always did. The only thing he failed to remember was the atom bomb that had been exploded over Hiroshima more than twenty five years ago. But in all fairness, no one could be expected to associate that long ago event with this robbery in Brisbane one generation later. Nevertheless, that bomb led to the failure of this well hatched plot.

Fred Hangler entered the bank, carrying a big briefcase in one hand, while the other firmly gripped a revolver —inside his coat pocket, of course. He was angry to note that several customers were present. The boss had counted on nobody wanting to transact any business at noontime, either depositing money or, worse still, taking out any sums. Well, there was nothing Fred Hangler could do about it now!

He walked to the end of the line of waiting customers. Only one window was still open for business. The teller behind the other, closed window was yawning. He glanced in a most disapproving manner at the new customer and then proceeded to unwrap his sandwich. A bottle of milk completed his frugal lunch.

In the meantime, his colleague was busy helping the four customers waiting for his services. He paid out one small sum to the first customer, gave some information to the second and then turned to the third man. Fred Hangler noticed with pleasure that his hypothetical fortune was just about to be increased by this obliging gentleman, who intended to deposit the tidy sum of several hundred pounds.

Fred's palm grew moist. He held on tightly to the gun in his pocket. The man in front of him began to count out the pound notes in a most laborious way. Just as slowly and meticulously were the same bills rechecked by the teller behind the window.

Suddenly the teller with the sandwich and the milk bottle

stopped eating his lunch and sat very still, as if listening to some voice that no one else could hear. A strange glimmer lit up his eyes. His glance wandered slowly around the room and, as if by accident, began to rest on Fred Hangler. A deep furrow formed between his eyebrows. Then he put his foot on the hidden alarm button.

Nothing happened in the bank. But just a short mile away, inside the nearest police station, sirens began to howl, startling the inspector from his midday snooze, which he had started prematurely. The hands of the wall clock were not yet pointing to 12. The inspector jumped up and stared at the alarm panel. Number 4 was lit up on it. That meant the Central Bank. Alarm. Robbery!

Bank robbery? Now, at *siesta* time? Unheard of gall of these criminals.

The inspector was seized by righteous indignation. He tore the receiver off the hook and began to bark some furious commands into the phone. Then he fastened his holster, made sure of the gun and ran out of the room. Outside in the corridor he met his alerted officers.

"Robbery in the Central Bank! Get a move on!"

Any thought of *siesta* time had vanished. A few seconds later a police car manned by five policemen were racing out of the police garage, siren whining, toward the Central Bank.

In the meantime, John Marshall had removed his foot from the silent burglar alarm button. He knew that it would be at most five minutes before the police would appear, unless they were fast asleep. One always had to reckon with such a possibility during the midday heat in this peaceful town. He did not take his eyes off the customer, who was now waiting quite patiently, until the man ahead of him had made his deposit and departed. Then the customer stepped close to the window.

The police inspector was smart enough to throttle the siren as he approached his destination. Without drawing any undue attention, the police car drove up close to the bank building and stopped on the other side of the road.

The same moment that the uniformed men jumped out of the police car, the big black limousine, which until now had been parked right in front of the bank entrance, drove off. There was nothing conspicuous about this, and nobody paid any particular attention to the departing limousine.

Fred Hangler placed the big briefcase on the counter ledge in front of him and said in a quiet voice, "Young man, I would like to make a withdrawal of all the money you have there in your safe. Here is my authorization to do so." With this he pulled the gun out of his pocket and aimed it at the teller. He risked one quick glance over at the teller at the next window. John Marshall sat calmly munching his sandwich and waiting for the next development, the arrival of the police.

"Don't touch the burglar alarm," the gangster warned Marshall. "You'd be a dead man before the cops had a chance to get here."

"I wouldn't be so sure of that," answered Marshall, chewing and taking another sip of milk. "Just turn around and see for yourself. The police are here already."

Hangler stared at him, completely beside himself. The first teller disarmed him deftly, before Hangler could offer any resistance. Hangler turned around. He saw five policemen quickly cross the road and enter the bank building.

The inspector was the first to storm into the bank. "What happened to the robbery?" he asked, nonplussed, and stopped in his tracks. He was confronted by a truly perplexing scene. Behind one of the tellers' windows somebody was sitting calmly eating a sandwich and drinking milk. The inspector hated milk passionately. In front of the other window he saw a harmless looking man who was being threatened by a gun held in the teller's hand. Just then, from a door in the background marked *Manager*, stepped a portly gentleman, hat in hand, ready to leave for lunch. He, too, stopped in his tracks, regarding the odd scene with disbelieving eyes.

"What's going on here, Myers?" he asked.

The bank teller, who kept pointing his pistol at Hangler, whispered excitedly, "What a coincidence! Good heavens, what a coincidence!"

"What coincidence?" inquired the inspector.

The bank manager came closer.

"He wanted to rob the bank," declared Myers. "Mr. Marshall tried to bluff him and pretended that the police were coming. The guy grew so nervous that I managed to disarm him. And then, what do you think? the police did come. I don't understand how it all happened."

"The burglar alarm was triggered," snorted the inspector. "Have you already forgotten about that button next to your feet?"

"I didn't give any alarm," insisted Myers. "And even if I had stepped on the burglar alarm, wouldn't it have been too late? This guy had hardly finished saying that he was holding me up, when you walked in here."

"Our police force just can't be beat," remarked the manager radiantly. He had come to believe that he had it all figured out.

In the meantime Hangler had regained his composure.

"You can't prove a darn thing!" he snapped insolently. "I always carry a weapon. All I came in here for was to withdraw some money."

"Yes, indeed," agreed Myers. "With a gun pointed at me."

"We'll soon enough find out the truth," interjected the inspector, and motioned to his men. Handcuffs closed tight around Hangler's wrists. "Be it as it may. Just three minutes ago we received an alarm signal at the station." He checked his watch. "To be exact, let's make it almost four minutes."

Myers looked at the clock. "Four minutes ago I was still serving another customer and didn't have the faintest notion of a holdup. Marshall over here had just started on his lunch break."

"Uhum!" The manager cleared his throat with noisy reproach. He shot a most disapproving glance at the second teller. "You arrive late in the morning but make up for it by going on an early break. And probably make overtime there! I sure like that," he concluded in a sarcastic tone.

"So do I!" John Marshall smiled back, unperturbed. "That's why I came here to work for you in the first place."

The bank manager's left eyebrow shot up at an angry angle. Myers grinned. The inspector gave Hangler a shove toward the door. "Let's go. We'll have plenty of time to discuss this." He looked over to the manager. "You should be pleased to have such reliable and prompt people working for you. But for them, you would have been out a lot of money. And for you, Mr." He hesitated. "Mr. Myers, I believe it is. I'd like you to come down to the station a bit later to make a sworn statement."

The inspector relieved Myers of the holdup man's gun, then led his small army out of the bank.

"What were you saying just now?" inquired the manager, and glanced with obvious disgust at the emptied milk bottle. He seemed to share the inspector's dislike for milk.

"I simply emphasized how much I like to work for you."

"Well, I'm glad to hear that!" He turned to Myers and continued, "My dear Myers, I would like to express my appreciation for your fast action. If you hadn't taken away that burglar's gun so quickly, and if you hadn't pushed the silent alarm button . . ."

"I didn't give any alarm," said Myers. "I only saw the police drive up and stop across the street and then run inside. That's when I could start acting. If anyone pushed that alarm button it must have been Marshall. But no, that's impossible too." He paused, then said, "The police could not have got here that fast. When that guy pulled out his gun, it was not more than five seconds later that the police showed up. I simply can't understand the whole thing," he concluded, shaking his head.

The manager apparently felt pity for his lonely raised left eyebrow, for he provided some company for it high up on his furrowed forehead.

"Mr. Marshall," he said curtly, "was it you who gave the alarm?"

"Why, of course, sir."

"The moment you saw the gangster point his gun at Myers?"

"No. Before that."

"Before that?" repeated the manager, confounded. His whole face looked like a question mark. "But how could you have known then what that man wanted to do? Or can you read minds?" he concluded with mockery.

Marshall nodded in silent affirmation. "It looks like it, doesn't it, sir? I knew exactly what this man intended to do. He was standing there in line, waiting for his turn. Then suddenly I was aware that he was holding a gun in his right hand, to threaten Myers. What else should I have done, for heaven's sake? I simply had to step on that alarm button. That's what it is here for, after all."

"Strange, most strange indeed." The bank manager scratched his skull, right at the spot where he had a few straggly hairs left. "You must have caught the brain radiations of this man. You must have received his thoughtwaves. Incredible! If it were not for the difference in time I wouldn't believe a single word you say. Have you ever experienced anything like this before?"

"What do you mean, sir?"

"Well, reading someone else's mind." He cleared his throat. "Do you know what I am thinking of now, Marshall?"

John frowned. Again he seemed to listen attentively to an inner voice. Then his face lit up. "Oh, how marvelous, sir."

"What would be marvelous?"

"The reward for Myers and myself." Marshall's face was shining with pleasure. "You were just thinking of giving us a bonus of 100 pounds, weren't you?"

The bank manager stared at him as if he had lost his mind. Then fear came into his eyes. As if trying to ward him off, he stretched both hands out against Marshall.

"That's uncanny, weird! A telepath! You are a telepath, Mr. Marshall! That's exactly what I was thinking of. To give you a reward! Good Lord, how could you have known?"

John Marshall smiled again and placed the empty milk bottle under the counter. He looked younger than his real age, especially when he was smiling. "I don't know, sir. At school I always knew everything better than any of the other students. I just *knew* the answers. Maybe because the teacher was thinking of them. But today, looking back at it, it seems that that must have been more than just guesswork."

"I am inclined to agree with you there!" mumbled the manager. "You should have yourself examined and tested by some experts, Mr. Marshall. You are a phenomenon. Incredible! If I had not witnessed the whole affair, I would never believe it."

Neither did anyone else believe it, naturally. Particularly the press. Though many articles were written about the foiled bank robbery with big headlines in the daily papers

—*Telepath unmasks Bank robber*—in reality no one took the whole story seriously. Only Jules Arnold and the boss worried about it. But what could *they* do, now it was too late?

That night John Marshall did not turn in as early as usual. He locked the door of his small bachelor apartment, went into the tiny kitchen, and prepared himself a snack. Then he settled down with half a bottle of brandy. He sat in his livingroom, which could be changed into a bedroom by pulling down a wall bed. Once again he let the events of the day pass in review in his mind.

Fred Hangler was a notorious gangster; that much he had learned from the evening newspaper. John had not especially noticed him when he first entered the bank; he had been too busy with his lunch. Then, something had suddenly crept into his mind. Yes, it had crept.

. . . must wait until the three ahead of me are through . . . Could be that they will deposit some money . . . that teller is no problem . . . Point my gun at him . . . boss outside . . . holdup.

Although John had not understood entirely, he had reacted with lightning speed There were four customers present. Therefore, the last one must be the gunman. That was only logical.

. . . damn it, he is withdrawing some money now . . .

John felt his flesh creep in horror. He could perceive so clearly the emotions of the fourth man waiting in line. Squinting slightly from behind his milk bottle, he observed the man out of the corner of one eye. Right hand in his pocket—that meant a gun, of course. Right. No doubt.

John had released the alarm.

. . . but this one is making a big deposit, at least! Just a few seconds now. Keep calm. . . .

Once upon a time John had been in love with a girl. It had often happened that he told her something that she was just about to tell him. They had said, "Our souls are swinging on the same wavelength."

. . . I hope no one else is going to come in now . . . Safety catch released . . . Soon . . .

Perhaps it was something like thought transference reflected John. If one was thinking very intensely, possibly

128

the delicate energy waves in his brain were a little stronger than usual and could be received by another person. Just the way a radio could receive the waves from a transmitter. John must be especially sensitive to thought waves; he must have a particular talent. But never had he experienced it as clearly as today. He was convinced that he could have caught all the gangster's thoughts if he had not been so excited. But the bank manager, on the other hand—how easy it had been when he had asked him to demonstrate his ability.

. . . and now . . . the gun . . . yes . . . now . . .

And then suddenly the police had appeared. John sighed. He had spent only a short time at the police station, being interrogated. He had signed his statement, and that was the end of his part in the whole affair. Mind reading! The inspector had scoffed at the idea and said something nasty about drinking too much milk. Too much stimulation of the brain, perhaps. But then he had thanked him and spoken about extraordinary ability for swift reaction. But Fred Hangler was sitting safely behind bars!

Perhaps this extraordinary ability could be perfected with the proper kind of training, John mused. So far he had paid little attention to it, had always thought it to be coincidence. But it could be that many other people felt the same who had similar talents. Telepathy had been described in many novels and in reports of scientific experiments, but nobody really believed in it. Well, John thought, he had ample proof today of its existence. He would have to investigate this a bit further, make some experiments of his own to see whether he could really read minds.

Wouldn't it be something if I could.

John began to spin daydreams. He could see himself as the eighth wonder of the world, whose favors would be eagerly sought after by politicians, giants of industry and the like. They all would want to have a telepath as an advisor, to outguess their competitors' intentions. Of course, they would pay him handsomely.

How about Miss Nelson in the apartment next door? wondered John. *She is home now; I saw her come in a little while ago. There is only a thin wall separating us. Thoughts can't be stopped by mere walls. I should give it a try . . .*

Suddenly he was seized by feverish excitement. Today's events had swept away any doubt he had had before. He could read thoughts, if he put his mind to it! Why had it never occurred to him before to test his ability? Now he could prove to himself that it was no mad dream or mere coincidence.

He got up and walked over to the wall.

He placed his ear against it and heard somone breathing quietly on the other side. Well, Miss Nelson must be in bed already. Maybe she was still reading, perhaps even the newspaper reports of the foiled robbery attempt at his bank. She should by now be aware what kind of hero was living next door to her.

John had never shown any special interest in Miss Nelson. She was young and pretty, and she worked as a salesgirl in some department store. They were good neighbors, nothing else, although John would not have minded if they had been a bit better acquainted.

All was quiet. John tried to concentrate. He imagined himself able to see the girl as she lay in bed. He tried to recognize her face as she looked at him . . . with admiration. And then . . .

It was as if John had received an electric shock.

At first he believed it to be nothing but imagination, but then his doubts vanished. Again it seemed as if strange thoughts were creeping into his brain and pushing aside his own thoughts. And then, not only could he understand these thoughts, but he began to see with the girl's eyes. He could see the book she was reading, the small bedside lamp beside her, even the lines in the book. He was able to read them clearly.

For an instant he closed his eyes. He was horrified—it was too much!—but the thoughts persisted. Now she laid down the book and went on thinking. How strange—she was thinking of him, of her neighbor John Marshall.

Good grief! What thoughts!

John blushed in embarrassment like a schoolboy and stepped back from the wall. He opened wide his eyes, fell into a chair and hid his face in his hands. And then he started to laugh.

It worked! It was not a figment of his imagination!

He was able to read other people's minds, if he concentrated on it. There was no longer any doubt about his gift.

But it would probably be wiser not to let anyone know about it, at least, for the time being. First he had to perfect his talent; then he could try to make money with it.

He completely forgot about the newspaper reports, which were ignored by most people but were taken seriously by a few.

But one thing he did not forget—to pay a friendly visit to Miss Nelson the next day.

Everything had happened quite differently in Miss Sloane's case.

Since her eighteenth year she had been aware that she was not what one considered a normal young girl. She had been told so by her father, a well-known atomic physicist, who had collaborated on the development of the first nuclear weapon. He lived now in retirement in Richmond, Virginia. Three months before Anne was born, her mother had accidentally been exposed to a strong field of radiation while visiting her husband in his lab. There had been no noticeable effects at first, but then after Anne was born, her father's attention was always focused on her.

When she reached the age of eight the first signs of deviation appeared. Driven by a strong desire, Anne had managed to set in motion an electric toy train, although it was not connected to any source of current. Her ardent wish to see the toy train move had started it and kept it driving around the toy tracks in her playroom. Professor Sloane had been horrified at first, but then he had realized that the atomic radiation to which Anne had been exposed before birth must have altered the structure of her brain. Faculties that normally lay dormant in that human brain had been awakened and developed.

Anne Sloane had the power of telekinesis.

What had been suspected for a long time became certainty in the ensuing years. When she turned eighteen her father enlightened her. From then on Anne began to observe herself systematically. She constantly discovered new variations of telekinesis and then fled to Europe under an assumed name to escape the investigations of well-known scientists. Systematically and quietly she began to train herself until she mastered matter by her sheer willpower.

Now she was twenty-six years old, the same age as John Marshall.

Now she had returned to Richmond, to live with her parents. She was respected and feared by her contemporaries. The President of the United States had personally guaranteed her safety. He had every reason to do so.

Anne was sitting on the veranda, taking a sunbath, when the two gentlemen in gray suits rang the doorbell. It was not the first time that such visitors had come. It was obvious to anyone, even at a distance, that they belonged to the secret service.

But this time things were somehow different.

Their car was parked in the quiet side street in front of the Sloane residence. Another car was waiting just behind the first auto. Four men were sitting inside. They had nondescript faces, but their eyes were extremely alert. They did not take their eyes off the house into which the two gentlemen had disappeared.

Anne's mother, too, noticed at once that her two visitors were not the usual type of special agent. They radiated authority and power. They must be quite high in the hierarchy of the secret service.

"We would like to talk to Miss Anne Sloane," said one of the gentlemen, a short and young looking man with already thinning hair that surrounded the bald dome of his head like a golden wreath. His gray temples heightened the impression he gave of a very peaceful person. "We have come on very important official business."

"I guess so," replied Mrs. Sloane, who by now was used to such callers. "Another order from our government, I presume. We have tried to avoid these things, not with too much success, unfortunately."

"The freedom of the whole Western world is more important than the convenience of a single individual," the man insisted solemnly. "This is indeed a most urgent matter."

"My daughter is outside on the veranda. Will you follow me, please?"

The second visitor looked older but radiated such kindness and joviality that one felt like addressing him right away as "uncle." He bowed courteously to Mrs. Sloane, and both gentlemen walked behind her, through the back of the house.

Anne was rather displeased when her mother announced the visitors. But as soon as she peered into the friendly yet firm eyes of her callers, her resistance melted away. Instinctively she knew that she was not dealing with run of the mill agents.

"You have left me alone for a little while," she remarked, as if in gratitude. She pointed to two chairs next to the small table near her. "Won't you have a seat, gentlemen, and then tell me what your trouble is? In the meantime my mother will get you something cold to drink."

She did not expect any introductions, for all her secretive visitors were called either Smith or Miller, or perhaps Jones. Quite frequently she had been able to assist the FBI or similar institutions with her unusual faculties. In return she enjoyed the protection of the government.

The younger of the two pulled up a chair and sat down. "My name is Allan D. Mercant, in case that should mean anything to you. I am chief of the International Intelligence Agency and also Chief of International Defense. May I introduce to you Colonel Kaats, Chief of the Inner Defense, a special department of the Federal Bureau of Investigation."

Anne half-closed her eyes. She was full of apprehension.

"I am very pleased to meet you, gentlemen, but isn't it rather unusual that you of all people should go to the trouble—"

"No trouble at all, Miss Sloane, but a genuine pleasure to finally meet our trusted collaborator in person. We have heard a great deal about you." Mercant moved his chair so that he could look directly into Anne's eyes. Kaats sat close to him. Mercant looked benevolently at the young girl. "But you can rest assured that this is not just a courtesy call."

"I thought not." She nodded lightly.

"We are in a predicament, and we need your help," urged Kaats.

"I am sorry to hear that." Anne looked up at the blue sky and wondered if she would ever again be as happy, gay and unburdened as she had been in her childhood. "Yes, I am listening."

Mercant cleared his throat. "The best thing will be to start right from the beginning. This will give you an idea what has happened and why we require your help. We are not confronted here by the usual problem. We are not searching for some spy or some other enemy agent. We are searching for something much more vital—peace for the world."

"You remember that once before I made the attempt—"

"Yes. I know about that. You wanted to force the big powers to destroy their atomic arsenals. That attempt was bound to fail, for force can be met only by some other force. But somebody else accomplished it. You know who that is, I assume. Perry Rhodan."

Yes. She had heard of him.

"Is your visit in any way connected with Perry Rhodan?"

"Yes. You are familiar with the story. Perry Rhodan, former major of our young space force, was leader of the first expedition to the moon. He was accompanied by Captain Reginald Bell, Lieutenant Eric Manoli and Captain Clark G. Fletcher. On her return flight to earth, the *Stardust* did not land as planned in Nevada but in the Gobi Desert. It seems that Rhodan found something on the moon that provided him with tremendous power. In the meantime we have learned that he encountered an extraterrestrial spaceship that had made a forced landing on the moon. These aliens have at their disposal the products of a technology that is advanced beyond the wildest imagination. At the time when war threatened to break out between East and West, Rhodan intervened in the conflict, calling himself the Third Power. He succeeded in keeping both enemies from annihilating each other. Certainly a most commendable enterprise; this much must be admitted.

"But at the same time this demonstration of power represents a tremendous potential danger. Just imagine, Miss Sloane—somewhere on Earth there exists a power capable of wiping out all the nations of this world. Perry Rhodan, unfortunately, is today in a position whereby he can impose his will on us. With the assistance of these aliens, he managed to foil to a certain degree the expeditions to the moon that were later undertaken together by us and the

Asiatic Federation. His might already extends, therefore, out into space. There is now such a concentration of power in the Gobi Desert as is hard to visualize. They are building spaceships and producing weapons, and no one on Earth can prevent it. Invisible energy screens extend around their installations, which are safe even from atomic bombs. In addition to that, they can manipulate gravity and control men's minds at a certain distance."

Mercant grew silent. He looked at Anne Sloane, full of hope. The girl seemed to ponder his last words.

"I must admit, this seems like a rather extraordinary and perhaps painful situation, but not menacing. Why should Rhodan be considered a danger to the human race? Didn't his intervention prove rather the contrary, that he had our best interests at heart, when he prevented an atomic holocaust?"

"Are you so sure of his motives?" countered Mercant. "No one really knows what is going on in the Gobi Desert. So far Rhodan refuses any explanation for his intervention. Still, his presence is of a definite advantage to us, inasmuch as it has pushed a war between East and West into the realm of fantasy. Even the most ardent enemies become allies when they are faced by a still mightier common foe. We are now cooperating with the secret services of the Asiatic Federation and the Eastern Bloc. But so far we have not met with any success. This is where you come in, Miss Sloane!"

"What am I supposed to do?" inquired Anne. "You know yourself the limitations of my capabilities. And besides, I haven't the faintest idea how this energy screen will react when someone tries to pierce it with thoughtwaves. And that I will have to do if I want to accomplish my task in a telekinetic way. Really, Mr. Mercant, I don't have the slightest notion how to proceed."

"You will naturally receive your instructions from us," declared Mercant, considering her words a partial consent. "We have even worked out a detailed plan of procedure for you. Our final aim is to render harmless Perry Rhodan and his superior weapons."

"Why must you do that? He has not done any harm to you. And isn't Rhodan a citizen of the United States?"

"He *was!*" emphasized Kaats. "He renounced his citizenship, and he has been deprived of all his rights. Perry Rhodan is the enemy of mankind."

Anne looked up again toward the sky. The sun had advanced and now approached the top of a big elm tree in her backyard. Soon shadows would fall onto the veranda.

"The enemy of mankind?" pondered Anne. "I have always imagined him to be somebody quite different—the man who prevented an atomic war."

Mercant grew restless. "My dear Miss Sloane, you must leave that to our judgment. We are better informed than you. Rhodan intends to seize not only this planet's military might but also its total economic potential. The machines and goods he can offer in trade already surpass anything we have ever dreamed of accomplishing. This alone is sufficient for Rhodan to shake the very foundations of our economic existence."

"That sounds great," she mocked. "I would like to meet this Rhodan very much. This makes your proposition sound acceptable to me."

"You will have an opportunity to make his acquaintance if you are willing to work with us," promised Mercant. "Perry Rhodan and his allies are looking for friends and helpers."

She was amazed. "How can this be possible? To seek friends while being known as the world's foremost foe? How does he go about it?"

"Quite openly. Who could prevent him from doing so? And how is anyone to guess his neighbor's destination when he packs his suitcases and leaves home? Dr. Haggard from Australia was abducted by force. Today he is working for Rhodan. We tried to smuggle in some of our agents, but they were caught. Maybe you will have better luck."

"I would seriously doubt that." Anne shook her head. "I can hardly believe I'd be more successful than your people, who are so much more experienced than I."

"That's just the point! Exactly because you have *less* experience. Our agents were too cautious and wary and reacted accordingly. Besides, you are a woman."

"I won't deny that," she smiled. "But what has that to do with the whole thing?"

"A good deal. One of the members of the *Stardust*'s crew wanted to return to the States. Rhodan gave him a hypno-block that induced an artificial amnesia. When Captain Fletcher was cross-examined by the Australian authorities, he unfortunately suffered a stroke. His widow died too a few weeks later, when her first child was born. Her death was kept a secret. But we are in possession of her papers. And we also have a photo of her. Have a look at it, Miss Sloane!"

Mercant opened his wallet and took out a photo. Anne hesitated slightly before she accepted the proferred picture; then she looked at it. It showed a young woman, about twenty-five years old, dark and slender. Anne did not notice anything particular about it except that it reminded her of somebody she knew quite well. . . .

"It looks like you, doesn't it?" asked Kaats eagerly.

Now Anne could see the resemblance, but it was nothing more than a slight likeness. "No one would dream of mistaking me for her, if that is what you want to say. No, I don't think I could pass for her."

"That is not so important here in this case," Mercant said. "Neither Rhodan, Bell nor Manoli had ever met Mrs. Fletcher in person. They might have seen a photo of her. Therefore, a slight resemblance is all that is necessary. As Mrs. Fletcher you will try to enter Rhodan's base in the Gobi Desert."

"This is a crazy idea," said Anne skeptically. "Who would fall for such a trick?"

"Rhodan! He will understand that Fletcher's widow wants to get in touch with him to find out what led to her husband's death. Once you are inside the energy wall, you can try out your special talents of telekinesis. I don't think even the fabulous Arkonides know a protection against that. At least, we hope they don't.

"Arkonides?"

"That is what the aliens call themselves. The strangers who had to make an emergency landing on the moon. They originate from a solar system more than 34,000 light-years away from ours. Star cluster M 13, NGC number 6205, to be exact."

"If these aliens really have come from this far distant

star, I'm afraid that my limited faculties won't impress them too much."

"Let's wait and see. In any case I am not wrong in assuming that this job sounds tempting to you? You do accept, I hope."

"I don't seem to have much of a choice. And besides, to be frank, this mission intrigues me."

Mercant rummaged in his coat pocket and pulled out some papers. "Here are your instructions. And your airplane ticket. But before you start you will undergo a short but intensive training course in psychology."

Suddenly Anne felt cold. She gazed up and noticed that the sun was now hidden by the branches of the elm tree. She stood up. "Let's go inside, it's too cool here on the veranda now. Over some whiskey you can explain all the details to me."

While she led the way into the house, she was suddenly overwhelmed by the feeling that she had let herself in for more than she could handle. Perry Rhodan, the celebrated astronaut, had gained her complete admiration when he had undertaken his daring flight to the moon. She had not been able to make much of the events that had followed, but she was sure that he was neither a traitor nor a criminal, even if the whole world was against him. And now all of a sudden she was supposed to fight against him.

She was not entirely sure that she really would.

Unlike Anne Sloane, Ras Tschubai had never had the slightest indication of his hidden talents. He was born a few years after the end of World War II in El Obeid, a tiny village in the Sudan. He had studied in India and had lived for the past two years in Moscow, the metropolis of the Eastern Bloc. He worked in the laboratory of a scientific institute involved in research into the production of a serum to prolong life.

As a chemist, Ras took part in an expedition into the interior of Africa where a particular species of bee could be found. Their liquid food was indispensable for the synthesis of the serum.

For weeks now the expedition had roamed the jungles near the headwaters of the Congo River, far from civilization and cut off from their supply sources. Radio communication with the outside world had been cut off when their radio stopped functioning. The native porters had taken French leave one after the other and had disappeared into the darkness of the jungle nights.

Their situation was desperate, for the slightest relapse into primitive circumstances meant certain ruin in this age of advanced technology. Both Russians, the German and the African born Ras Tschubai were sitting in the middle of the immense jungle, surrounded by virgin territory and hostile wilderness, far removed from any help. What irony when high above the dense roof of foliage they could hear the hum of the heavy transcontinental airplanes! Just a few miles above them, yet unreachable.

They ran out of food as well as medical supplies.

The leader of the misfortune ridden expedition sighed, "Damn these wonder bees! Prolonging life! For that we don't need any bees now, just a few cans of food. And a lot of luck. Ras, you are the only one here who knows this country at all. If anyone can help us now, it's you."

They were crouched around a small campfire in front of their tent. The fire was smoking terribly, for they had been able to find only damp wood. The sun never penetrated as far down as the jungle floor.

"I was only born in Africa but educated in India and the Soviet Union," Ras replied.

"But your parents lived here and your ancestors. You inherited their knowledge and their instincts. You are the only one who could find a way out of this maze. We have tried in vain for days to reach even some village. We have not enough strength left to carry on. One of us must go on alone. You, Ras!"

Ras was frightened. It was correct that his grandparents and even his parents had fought in Africa against the white man for their freedom and independence. They had lived in these endless steppes and impenetrable jungles. They had found food by hunting the animals of their domain. But he was now one generation removed from them. What did he know of the dangers of this wilderness? Nothing.

He shook his head in desperation. "It is senseless; that much I know. I'll never find the way on my own. Who knows if there is anybody still living in this jungle? They are all concentrated now near the coast or on the steppes. Even the wild tribes were lured by civilization. The jungle has been deserted. The wild animals have taken over. How should I, a man alone, find my way back to civilization?"

As he spoke, a picture appeared before him from days long gone by. He saw El Obeid, a tiny oasis in the wide Sudanese steppes that had developed first into a little village and then into a regular small town. El Obeid! That was where his parents had lived, where he had been born. Here he had spent his childhood, those long ago days without any worries. The village school and the teachers and the funny memories of many a childish prank . . . The old chieftain who used to sit under a banana tree at the edge of the village pond and who told such interesting stories . . . How well Ras could remember all this, just as if it had been only yesterday. And his parents . . .

"Instinct, Ras!" said the leader of the expedition, bringing Ras back to reality. "It isn't the compass that matters but the instinct. Your parents were still savages when they were children, don't you ever forget it. Your own civilization is nothing but a thin veneer that can be stripped away at any time. Forgive me if that sounds rather brutal, but it's the truth. It takes many generations to turn this thin layer into a thick and durable skin. You, Ras, belong to the first generation. If anyone of us has a chance for survival, it is you. Therefore, you are the one to go for help."

Slowly Ras looked around the campfire. The German was squatting close by. He seemed to be cold, although it was warm and humid. He was drying his feet and boots, which had become soaked in the swamp. One of the Russians was sitting on a rotting tree trunk, staring straight ahead with a somber expression. His rifle was leaning next to him, but only two bullets were left in it. The leader of the expedition regarded Ras expectantly.

The student of chemistry sighed deeply. "You're the boss. If you want me to, I'll try my best. But I can't guarantee anything."

"That remains to be seen. Take this rifle here and five rounds of ammunition. That will leave us ten bullets for hunting. In addition here is your share of medications. It's not much, but it will do for one fever attack. You will have to hunt for your food."

"That means no food to take along?"

"That's right. We can't give you any! We have almost nothing left. I am sorry, but I can't see any other way out. You must start out today."

Ras knew that he could not argue; it would be senseless. He obeyed orders and soon afterward took his leave from his comrades. He walked off with firm steps and soon disappeared into the dense underbrush of the jungle. The thick foliage closed behind him and hid his friends from view. They remained behind, sitting motionless in the little clearing, just staring after him.

At first things were not too bad. Ras found a path apparently made by wild animals on their way to a waterhole nearby. He followed the trail. *If I should continue like this for about 600 miles,* he thought bitterly, *I would reach the coast. The only problem is that it would take weeks or months at this speed. It is hopeless. But what can I do? Perhaps I'll be lucky and I'll find some nomadic tribe or some Pygmies. Or . . .*

El Obeid!

If only he had stayed there, everything would have been fine. Although he could not have studied, he would still have had a chance to live a long life. Perhaps he would even have become a teacher. His parents would still be alive, perhaps. As it was, only one sister lived in their old home. How long since he had last seen her!

Caution!

It was nothing but a monkey who, high up in the leafy roof of the jungle, had discovered the strange wanderer. His loud chatter aroused a lively echo. Ras was contemplating whether he should shoot him, but he did not feel hungry even though he had eaten hardly anything today. With a brisk step he continued on his way.

Soon it grew dark. Under no circumstances, he decided, would he spend the night down on the ground. He had to find some tree whose lowest branch was within easy reach. But this was not so easily done. It was almost night before he discovered a huge fallen tree trunk lying at a slant in a small clearing in the thick underbrush. He ran upward along the trunk until he reached a big forked branch, whence many paths led into a new realm that had been unknown to him till now. An entanglement of many branches, boughs and twigs wove a cover more than sixty feet above the jungle floor.

It was not at all difficult to find a suitable place. A cave-like leafy shelter provided protection against the night wind and cover against any enemies approaching from behind. He took the blanket roll he had carried on his shoulders and spread it out. Carefully he put the gun in a corner. He still felt no hunger, only great fatigue. He stretched out in a shallow depression of his "nest," listened for a while to the nocturnal noises of the primeval forest and was soon asleep.

He dreamed. Strangely enough, he dreamed of the scene of his childhood, of which he had thought earlier. He could see everything so clearly that it seemed to be reality. The old chieftain once again told his stories of those by-gone days when he roamed through the steppes, armed with spear and bow, hunting for enemy warriors and for game. Ras's sister brought water from a nearby well, carefully balancing the jug on her head. His parents—

Ras sat up with a start. A new sound, which so far had not been part of the nocturnal concert of the jungle, had awakened him from his dream.

At first the trunk had trembled lightly, as if something had jumped on it from the ground below. Then came a soft shuffling, as if the creature was cautiously approaching. Something was softly treading on the wood.

Ras reached for his gun. He could not find it at once, and while searching for it he knocked it over. Before he managed to get hold of it, it flipped over the edge of his tiny platform. He could hear the rifle hitting against branches and leaves on its downward path. A dull thud announced that his weapon had arrived on the ground.

Silence.

Ras trembled with fright. He was seized by a superstitious fear. Again the creeping, groping in the dark became audible. It seemed to be louder now.

And then suddenly . . . his heart stopped beating for a

moment. He saw two glowing lights close by. It must be a big jungle cat that had followed his scent.

Ras knew that he did not have a chance. His only weapon was lying far below him on the ground, perhaps even in the morass. His knife was very small, not of much use. How could he fight off a dangerous wild animal with it? But it was his only weapon, and he pulled it from his belt with shaking hands.

The two luminous eyes had apparoached him to a distance of less than ten feet. He could almost smell the stinking breath of his adversary, still hidden by the darkness. Ras remained sitting up straight, his back braced against the hollowed out tree trunk. He waited.

From the left something hissed viciously. The shining eyes in front of him suddenly disappeared, as the big cat attacked its rival on the left. Ras could see nothing but he could visualize the struggle that went on nearby in total darkness. Both animals were fighting for their prey. They were fighting over him.

The victor would not wait long before attacking him. There were still a few minutes left to him to prepare himself for the coming onslaught. There was not really very much he could do, he knew. His hand closed tight around the small knife.

The wild hissing of the battling animals seemed to move away a short distance, but it increased in ferocity and loudness. Claws tore at wood and caused a nerve-racking sound that chilled Ras to the marrow of his bones. And then, suddenly and unexpectedly, all became silent. But only for a fraction of a second. Then Ras could hear branches breaking, the sound of something bumping against foliage and trunk. This could only mean that one of the animals had lost its grip and fallen to the ground. The struggle was over.

Soon another would begin.

Once again he perceived the flickering eyes, a little farther away. Now they started moving toward him.

Damm it, why had he had to take such a tremendous risk! How could the leader of the expedition simply decide that Ras should walk through the jungle, all alone and almost unarmed? What on Earth had possessed him to emigrate to

Moscow? He should have stayed in El Obeid, with his parents and his sister.

Oh Lord, his sister! She was the only member of his family still alive. He had always been so fond of her. The house . . .

He forgot all about the wild animal that was slowly creeping nearer. If he had to die, then at least he would meet death thinking of his beloved home and his sister.

He could see her now in front of him in the small room in the back of the house. She sat at the table, grinding some grain to a fine flour. He was standing near the door, the way he had done at his last visit, just two years ago. She had not known that he was supposed to arrive and had not recognized him immediately. But then . . .

He would give anything now to be at her side this very second, to be in the safe shelter of the house. With all his might he longed for it, willed it. He could think of nothing else. He had even forgotten the wild cat. . . .

His sister was sitting at the table but she was not grinding any grain. Instead she was leafing through some letters she had taken from a box in front of her. Then she looked up and noticed Ras standing at the door. But this Ras was like a stranger she did not know. A disheveled man in torn clothes, with a knife in his right hand, raised high, ready for attack . . .

"Ras! What is the matter? Your knife . . ."

The chemistry student stood as if frozen. With wide-open eyes he stared at his sister. Slowly his hand came down, still holding the knife. He released his grip, and the knife fell to the floor with a clanking sound.

"Brother, what is wrong with you?"

Ras was breathing hard. He looked around the room, without comprehending how he had got here. Just a short second ago he had been sitting on a tree in the middle of the jungle more than a thousand miles away, facing a certain death.

And now . . .

El Obeid! His parents' house! His sister!

"Sara, is it really you? Am I really here?"

"Of course you are here. But what you look like! Did you escape? Did you break out from a prison?"

"Maybe I have done that," he murmured, trembling. "Maybe I escaped from a mental prison, from the barriers erected by my mind. But that can't be possible! Why me, of all people?"

"What are you talking about, Ras? I don't understand."

"Sara, I don't understand it myself. I don't know how I got here. I was far away in the jungle with an expedition. The expedition!" Suddenly he remembered what he had set out to do. They had sent him to get help. But now they were more than a thousand miles away. But . . . no, this no longer presented any problem. As long as he knew their exact location . . . Perhaps by airplane?

"Listen, Sara, my friends are in danger. I left them half a day ago . . . in the Congo."

His sister looked at him greatly worried. Ras was suffering from some fever attack. She must get him to a doctor as quickly as possible.

"Do you have some food in the house?" Ras asked firmly. "Make a bundle ready. Hurry up, please."

Ten minutes later he held a big bundle of food under his arm.

"Turn around now, Sara. I'll be back in about an hour. You must believe me, trust me. I shall . . ."

She ran past him toward the door and locked it. Then she hid the key in the pocket of her apron.

"You'll just stay here, Ras!" she cried, turning to close the window. "Whatever you are planning to do will have to wait until Dr. Swartz can come by to examine you. He will know—"

She did not finish her sentence. She had been turned away from him for only a moment, but when she looked back again toward Ras, all she saw was an empty spot where he had been standing with his bundle.

And a fourth case must be reported, for it was the most incredible and most baffling incident. It lay in the realm of parapsychology and concerned a special faculty, unknown so far. Nobody on Earth would have seriously considered such a possibility. . . .

Every Friday a few young artists from Schwabing, the

artists' quarter in Munich, Germany, gathered in the apartment of author Ernst Ellert. Each visitor brought along his own contribution to the evening's refreshment in the form of a bottle of wine or some salami. This gave each the reassuring feeling that they would not cause too much hardship on the small budget of the freelance writer.

This particular Friday they were celebrating the birthday of Jonny, a painter who was so possessed by his love of painting that he could not refrain, even tonight, from making a few sketches on the gaily colored wallpaper. Ellert had long since given up reprimanding him for such unwanted displays of his art. All he would hear for the rest of the evening would be Jonny's comments of "narrow minded frustrator of artistic creativity, the eternal curse of the true artist."

Late, as usual, Heinrich Lothar arrived; nobody knew for sure how he earned his living. There were rumors that he photographed models for magazines, did occasional translations and the like. All these occupations, however, never prevented him from taking each of his friends aside sometime during the evening and discreetly whispering, "Say, you couldn't lend me a fiver till tomorrow?" This most touching approach had only once been crowned by success, when Ellert had let himself be victimized. Of course, he had never seen his money again.

The fourth member of the group was Aarn Munro, editor and publisher of a small magazine that was read by hardly anybody. Aarn Munro was not his real name, naturally. But he liked to be called by the same name as the hero of a well-known science fiction novel of his youth. Since he could not make a living from his auctorial work alone, he had some other job, which he preferred not to mention. He'd rather be regarded as an artist, even if he never sold anything. And he did make excellent drawings.

Finally there was Frettel, who also was smart enough to regard his artistic activities as a sideline. Frettel was a singer, entertainer, manager, organizer, impresario and general patron of the arts, not to overlook his being a physician.

"Tonight's topic," began the host, swiftly extracting a cigarette from Aarn's pack when Aarn's attention was momentarily diverted, "came up for discussion last week. You remember that Frettel mentioned some strange happenings that are supposed to have occurred in London. We could not come up with a plausible explanation. Lothar thought these phenomena were due to one of the parasciences. To be honest, I don't know too much about them and therefore don't believe in them. At least, that was my opinion up till yesterday."

Lothar took the olives that Aarn had brought and unthinkingly emptied the contents of the small jar into the wide cavern of his mouth. He chewed on them with a great deal of enjoyment.

"Up till yesterday?" He ate and talked at the same time. "What do you mean by that?"

"That I have changed my opinion," replied Ellert, and tried without much success to rescue one of the olives for himself. He made up for this with a shot of the whiskey that Jonny had donated. "After all, artists are permitted to change their points of view if it pleases them. They don't have to be consistent."

"You are right; opinions are the only thing we can change," observed Frettel thoughtfully. "Besides the figures on our patients' monthly statements."

"You are a doctor!" pointed out Ellert to him. "Writers can't play that game so easily. Our publishers—"

Aarn was not at all interested in these problems. He simply did not pay anything for his writers' contributions to his magazine, for most writers were overjoyed just to see their names and their stories published. Therefore, he interrupted his friends' conversation rather abruptly. "Ernst, how come you waited until yesterday to think differently about parapsychology?"

Ellert was glad to get away from the unpleasant discussion about financial matters. Money was always a sore point with him. "Because something strange happened to me yesterday."

"Let's hear about it!" urged Jonny, while trying to save at least some of his drink for himself. "Maybe I'll get some new ideas from you."

"I can hardly believe that," countered Ellert with a good humored wink at Jonny. But at once he became serious again. "All right, I'll tell you a story, a most interesting story. But I know beforehand that no one will believe me."

He waited until his guests had settled down comfortably in their seats and lit their cigarettes. Then he asked, "What do you think of time travel?"

General bewilderment. Then Aarn snapped, "That's your hobby, isn't it? You even wrote about it once, and it wasn't too well received by sensible people. If you want me to be frank with you, I consider time travel a most entertaining fairy tale."

The rest of the group nodded unanimous agreement.

Ellert sighed. "That's what I expected you to say. But despite that, will you listen to my story, please! As you all know, I have pondered a great deal about this particular notion. I think it quite possible to go time traveling in a mental fashion. A dream could be looked upon as a kind of mental trip through time, if it transports us into either the past or the future. Even when you mentally recall events of the past you could speak of this as time travel to a certain limited degree. I think you will agree, therefore, that the notion of time travel is not so absurd as it might appear at first glance."

"Just a moment!" interjected Frettel. "That doesn't make sense! What has that to do with time travel? As I understand it, it consists of physically transferring the body of a person into the future or the past. Therefore, I would have to exist in some epoch different from my own, at least temporarily, in order to be able to speak of time travel."

"You are quite right," admitted Ellert, much to Frettel's surprise. "I share this view, although I tried to describe the other variation. In any case," he continued, "I've lain awake many a night trying to figure out how one could possibly have a glimpse of the future, even if I could do this only mentally without being physically transferred to some other era. I've racked my brain to understand the connection between dream, fantasy and wishful thinking; the relationship of the hypothetical eventuality of *tele*portation and *temporal* portation. Temportation, to coin a word. If we assume the possibility that the body can follow the mind to another location, then it should also be feasible for the body to follow the mind to another period in time."

"Oh boy!" admired Jonny, without letting go of his almost empty bottle on the table. "It's simply snorky the way you can make plausible some things that are really impossible."

"No wonder," grumbled Frettel. "That's what he gets paid for."

Ellert waited until the general excitement subsided. He looked very confident of himself now, and his good friends knew this to be the sign that he was going to spring some more surprises.

"It's getting interesting bit by bit," remarked Lothar with sarcasm.

"Go on with your story!" demanded Aarn, his eyes shining with speculation and full expectation.

Ellert did not need any urging. "I have always been interested in the future, and it seems that I have been constantly preoccupied with it. Especially so yesterday. Nobody knows what is going to happen tomorrow, and who is sure that he will exist the next day? In the last year we have had a few narrow escapes from an atomic Armageddon. Everybody understands the consequences of an atomic war. And if a certain Rhodan had not intervened, none of us would be sitting here so comfortably talking and drinking.

"But despite Rhodan's service to all mankind, he is looked upon as our enemy. This doesn't make sense to me. It's plainly illogical. Well, to make a long story short, last night before going to sleep, I directed my thoughts toward the future with such intensity that I almost believed I had arrived in it. I so fervently wanted to learn what would happen in one year. And then suddenly: I knew it!"

"I beg your pardon?" squeaked Jonny in utter amazement. He released his grip on the bottle for an instant, which was not lost on Aarn, who took the opportunity to help himself to the meager remainder of liquid refreshment. "You knew it? Be more specific, please!"

"I am just about to. While my thoughts were focused on the problem most intently, I suddenly noticed some change taking place. I could not define what kind of change this was, for everything seemed to happen so swiftly. It became dark in my room, for a few seconds or an eternity, who knows? Then all of a sudden it was daylight. The sun was shining bright. I was sitting here on my bed, wondering what had taken place that would account for the sudden turning of night into day."

"You must have had too much to drink," suggested Jonny.

Ellert shook his head. "Just wait a minute, my friend. I have not yet finished telling my story. Well, it was broad daylight, and the sun was shining. I got up from my bed and looked around, wondering all the while. At first I assumed that my mental effort had made me fall asleep abruptly and that morning had come and it was time for me to get up. Then I noticed that two of my pictures were missing from the wall. Yours, by the way, Jonny. Instead there were two new paintings, signed by Aarn . . ."

"But I have never drawn any pictures this size," objected Aarn.

"That's just the point!" exclaimed Ellert. "This is my first proof already. You are *going to paint* them—not draw them! And you will make me a present of them in the near future."

"He's gone off his rocker," whispered Lothar worriedly to Frettel, who was sitting next to him. "Why don't you examine him sometime?"

"I deal in appendix operations, not in brain abnormalities," said the physician without emotion.

Ellert did not seem to mind their discussing his state of sanity. "At first, of course, I did not understand. I examined the paintings more closely—and I may say I liked what I saw, Aarn—and walked toward the corner, where I stopped in front of my big wall calendar. You know this big calendar over there where I write down all my appointments. And what do you think I saw there on my calendar?"

"I haven't the faintest idea," mumbled Lothar. "But don't keep us in suspense. Go on speak!"

"The date! Why, what else should I see on my calendar? But it was the 17th of November two years hence!"

Jonny burst out laughing and kept laughing till tears came into his eyes. He tried to utter a few words, but they were unintelligible.

Frettel did not join in the general amusement; he remained serious. "Is that the truth?" he asked. "Explain! What happened?"

"A simple explanation might be that my almost super-humanly felt desire had brought me into the future, more than two years ahead in time. But the most amazing thing was that my body remained in the present time. At first I believed that my body, too, had arrived in the future, but then I noticed suddenly that another will was fighting against my own. I realized quickly that my own will of today was struggling with my will of two years hence. Only my mind had traveled into the future and slipped into the body of Ernst Ellert of two years from now. With *his* eyes I saw and experienced that period which is still lying ahead of us. I could even participate in the memories he had accu-mulated during these two years. But I did not succeed in imposing my will on his. Yet I knew that that same night our usual gathering was scheduled to take place, al-though according to the calendar it was a different day than we usually meet now. It was an exception. I was on leave, and this way we were able to get together for the evening."

"On leave," mused Jonny, as if he had never before heard such a word.

But Ellert did not care to elaborate on what kind of a leave he was on. Instead he reassured them. "I will set your minds at ease. All of us will still be alive in two years. No war will have broken out but tremendous changes will have taken place."

"Now I know what is ailing you, my friend," interrupted Lothar triumphantly. "He is taking up fortune telling."

"You might have a point there. Maybe that's what hap-pens with prophets when they start foretelling the future—perhaps they can send their minds some years ahead and report what they saw." Ellert sighed with resignation. "But I see you don't believe a word of my story."

"Of course we don't," smiled Frettel. "But it still is a most entertaining tale. I keep waiting for the punch line."

"Punch line?"

"Why, what else? It's a gag, isn't it?"

Ellert lit a cigarette. His face was very serious. "There

is no gag, there is no punch line. The story is simply the truth. Would you like me to prove it to you?"

"That would be nice of you," admitted Lothar. Frettel and the rest nodded in agreement. They looked at Ellert with great expectation.

"All right, my friends, I'll try now to attend our next Friday night party here. In other words, I'll be able to tell you right away what will happen in one week. Or even better still, what will occur during the coming week. I'll listen in to your usual weekly report of your activities at our next meeting by sending my mind ahead into the body of Ernst Ellert, one week older. Then I'll return and tell you all about it. Within the following seven days you will have ample opporunity to verify the correctness of my prediction. Are you with me?"

"You bet," grinned Frettel. "And in the meantime, while your mind has wandered off into the future, I'll examine your body right here in the present. Perhaps I might observe some difference in your body, and this will be an additional proof."

"I sincerely doubt that you will notice anything different in him," remarked Aarn in a highly critical tone.

Ellert paid no attention to this dispute among his friends. He leaned back in his armchair, head thrown back, eyes closed. He had stopped moving. His breathing was calm and regular. Frettel was waiting for any sign of change but could observe none whatsoever. Finally, growing impatient, he poked his index finger at Ellert's chest.

"Have you started with it, Ellert?" he inquired.

Ellert did not reply. He was sleeping. He could not be aroused. All attempts at awakening him failed. Frettel checked his pulse, heartbeat and blood pressure. All vital signs seemed to function perfectly, exactly the way they would in a sleeping person, except that this slumber was far deeper than anything the physician had witnessed before.

"He has been asleep now for five minutes like this," Frettel said, looking at his watch.

Johnny had turned serious too. He looked at Lothar and Aarn. "Do you believe there could be something to what Ellert has told us?"

They shrugged.

Suddenly Ellert opened his eyes. He looked around the room in confusion. Then he seemed to remember. He smiled weakly.

"Well?" urged Aarn. "What happened?"

"I was one week ahead in the future," whispered Ellert with resignation. "Exactly one week from now, from this very moment. For five minutes. But I can't tell you what will happen to you during this coming week. I did not see any of you. Apparently we won't meet here in my apartment Friday night. I did find my body, though, which had become one week older in the meantime. But not here in Munich."

"Where did you locate it?"

"In Asia! To be exact, in the Gobi Desert. How I got there, who knows? I don't at this point. It was difficult enough for me to get hold of a newspaper so I could at least tell you the events of the coming week. I wanted to bring some proof along to you of my trip into the future. Unfortunately, I could not transport the newspaper back with me, since I cannot cause *matter* to travel through time. But I did read some news items."

"Well, how about some tips on the stock market?" scoffed Jonny, who remained as skeptical as before. "I'd like to know why you were in the Gobi Desert, of all places. That's the spot where the American spaceship landed, isn't it?"

"You are right. It landed there. And in one week I'll be standing in front of the astronaut Perry Rhodan."

"Charming story," mocked Lothar. "Now I presume you will write one of your science fiction stories around this visit."

All the friends laughed, as if they had heard a good joke.

Only Ellert remained serious. "You won't be laughing in a few more days. I'm afraid there exists more things between heaven and Earth than we have imagined. The day after tomorrow will be our elections. I already know the result. Would that be enough proof for you doubting Thomases?"

Frettel narrowed his eyes.

"Certainly—if sheer coincidence could be ruled out."

Ellert shook his head. "True. The result of the election could be correct just by chance. But not the fact that the newly elected official will become the victim of a heart attack the very same evening. The elections will have to be repeated in another four weeks."

All fell silent. Then Aarn's soft voice could be heard:

"Telepathy, teleportation, telekinesis, and now to top it off we have teletemportation—travel through time. But only for the mind."

Frettel shouted with enthusiasm, "Ellert, you have invented a new branch of the parasciences!"

Ellert gave him a penetrating look.

"I *discovered* something that must have existed all along. I did not *invent* this phenomenon, my dear Frettel!"

CHAPTER FIVE

PERRY RHODAN thought that his eyes had been closed for just a brief moment. When he opened them again, nothing seemed to have changed. His friend Reginald Bell was lying strapped into the indoctrinator next to him, and he, too, was trying to wake up. There was an expression of utter amazement on his face.

The indoctrinator! Now suddenly Rhodan knew how it fuctioned. Stored data were conducted through electronic amplifiers, then transmitted directly into the nerves of the head. They in turn conveyed the information into the brain, where it was stored in the memory bank. These memory banks, though, had been considerably enlarged in their storing capacity via electric shocks. From there the accu-mulated wealth of knowledge could be tapped whenever needed.

Khrest stood at the instrument panel of the indoctrinator. "You may get up now!" he said quietly. "The hypnotraining has been successfully concluded. Both of you have received the identical schooling, but it seemed advisable to me to equip you, Perry, with a certain type of superiority, compared with what Reg has been given. I have increased your already present potential for lightning fast decision making in the face of newly arising situations. In addition to that your suggestive powers have been augmented. Any normal person will from now on have to carry out any of your commands, as if he had been given a hypnotic order. I am fully certain that you will never abuse this power entrusted to you. But you will have to make use of it in order to accomplish what we have planned together. As to the extent of your newly acquired knowledge, well, you will soon enough find out for yourself."

Rhodan pushed his hair away from his forehead. "Right now I am not aware of any change."

Khrest smiled gently. "What is the square root of 527,076?"

"Seven hundred and twenty-six. Why?"

Perry gave the result as nonchalantly as if it were the most elementary problem in arithmetic. But he had hardly finished with his reply, when he turned pale. He had already got up, and now he was so shaken by surprise that he seemed to lose his balance for a moment.

Reg grasped his arm to steady him. "I also know the answer!"

"Your brain calculates automatically at the speed of light, if I may make such a comparison," Khrest enlightened them. "Your calculations are taking place in your subconscious. Your conscious mind is needed for more important tasks. Are you convinced by now that something has been changed in you?"

Reg still seemed beside himself. "And my math teacher used to tell me that I would never amount to anything, at least not in math! If only he could see me now . . ."

"For the next few days you will constantly make new discoveries of what changes have occurred in you. Don't

155

be frightened by it. The only thing that matters is that you know how you have acquired your talents, that they were transmitted by our indoctrinator, based on the far advanced state of development of our race. You share our level of progress."

"I hope we will be able to handle it successfully."

"You will have to. And now, will you come along with me? I must discuss some things with you. Our connection with the outside world has been interrupted. Powerful transmitters are jamming our broadcasts and rendering impossible our contact with anyone else we need to communicate with. One of you will have to leave the protective energy dome to find out what is going on. Besides, we cannot afford to sit around inactive. The first worksheds have been erected. The robots cannot continue with their work. We must get materials and co-workers. We will build here in the middle of the desert an industrial complex the like of which your planet has not seen before. You realize that we will never get back to Arkon without powerful spaceships, and we want to accomplish more than just returning home, as you know."

Rhodan listened to Khrest's words. At the same time he mentally let pass in review the bold visions of the future of which Khrest had spoken to him. The galactic empire. A gigantic fleet would be required to build it up and to maintain it. But was mankind quite ready for this?

"I'll go outside myself," he heard himself volunteer to Khrest. "I only wonder how long it will be before they detect who I am."

"Well?" countered Khrest with eager anticipation. "Just think of the technical means at your disposal now, Perry."

And Rhodan realized this very instant what they were. The information simply came up from the memory bank of his augmented brain potential.

The Arkonide equipment. A microreactor supplied the energy of his special suit. He could erect a miniature energy screen around himself that would provide protection against any dangers. Small missiles would simply bounce off it. The lightwave deflector would render him invisible to human eyes. The built-in gravity neutralizer would permit flight for short distances, since the speed would remain fairly moderate.

"How will I be able to leave here?"

"Tonight we will lift the energy screen barrier for a few seconds, although you could pass directly through it if you wished to do so. But before that I would like to discuss the further details with you. Thora has agreed to this plan. She has come to understand the necessity for such a collaboration between us, even if most reluctantly."

"I am not surprised," said Rhodan curtly.

Los Angeles. Two days later.

In a small restaurant on Sepulveda Boulevard, the street leading to the international airport, Perry Rhodan sat enjoying a good sized steak. In the past two days he had managed to have talks with the presidents of three of the largest industrial concerns in the United States. Because of his new talents he had at once received confirmation for deliveries in the near future of large orders of the materials and manpower he needed. He had given a fictitious firm name in Hong Kong, under which he would accept delivery.

Outside the restaurant he had a taxi waiting for him to finish his meal.

Perry Rhodan sat quite calmly in the midst of a population that regarded him as their worst enemy. He was unafraid and did not even try to hide. Although his photograph had been telecast all around the world after his landing in the Gobi Desert, nobody seemed to have recognized him so far. And even if they did, it would not matter too much . . . Rhodan felt well protected by his Arkonide equipment. Underneath his business suit he wore a special suit, one that was undetectable from the outside.

A man sat down at the table next to Rhodan. His dark hair was combed back straight from his forehead. He looked rather distinguished, perhaps too much so. Large sunglasses hid his eyes. He opened a newspaper and soon seemed absorbed in it. He was reading the financial section. Absentmindedly he ordered some coffee.

Perry Rhodan tried to concentrate on his delicious steak, trying to overcome a sudden feeling of unrest. Two days had passed since he had left the base in the Gobi Desert. This apparent calm was suspicious.

What if they now launched the long expected general attack? Rhodan was convinced that the Arkonides would manage to ward off any attack from the enemy outside, but he feared a rash action on Thora's part. Unless she was watched she was liable in her wrath to cause the greatest catastrophe and thus to endanger all Khrest's and Rhodan's plans for the future. During yesterday's negotiations Rhodan had noticed that people were not absolutely against him. On the contrary, the farsighted industrial magnates had recognized the advantages that their association with Rhodan offered them. In addition, each was fully aware that Rhodan's actions and the existence of his base in the Gobi Desert had prevented an atomic war.

Rhodan wondered how his friend Reginald Bell would react in the face of an attack from the outside world. Now he possessed incredible intelligence and new, undreamed of capabilities, but his character remained unchanged. Not that Reg liked to act unthinkingly, but he needed Rhodan's presence to counterbalance his impulsiveness.

The gentleman at the next table had put down his newspaper. There were deep creases in his forehead now. His attention was obviously focused on his neighbor, who had just finished eating and pushed away his empty plate. Several times he seemed to want to get up from his seat, but he apparently could not quite make up his mind. Then finally he stood up abruptly and walked over to Rhodan's table.

He stopped short for an instant, looked at Rhodan and then said, "Pardon me, sir, I would like to ask you something, if you don't mind. May I sit down?" Before Rhodan could give his assent the stranger had pulled up a chair and sat down next to him.

Rhodan was startled by his behavior and was mentally prepared for anything that might follow, even a physical attack. A slight push on his belt would have been sufficient to surround him with a protective energy bell.

The stranger smiled uneasily. "I might be mistaken, but two things speak against this. True, the resemblance is rather vague, but I could swear I have seen you somewhere before. But this is not the only reason I suspect that you are Perry Rhodan. Please, don't be afraid—you have nothing to fear from me. I would not give you away. You have done too much good for all of us on Earth. But I don't know how to tell you, Mr. Rhodan. Don't you read any newspapers?"

Rhodan shook his head. "Not in general. Just for the last two days, though . . ."

"No, sir. It was about a week ago that a lot was written in the papers about me, at least in Brisbane, Australia, where I am from. No one would believe what had happened, but it was absolutely true. I am John Marshall, if that name means anything to you."

Rhodan remembered having heard something about this man, but he had dismissed it from his mind at once as being inconsequential. Just some sensational bit of news, that was all. But swiftly the report assumed some importance. His logically working mind went into action and within a fraction of a second gave an answer to why this man had been able to identify him as Perry Rhodan. He raised his eyebrows.

"You are the mind reader, Mr. Marshall. You were sitting here next to me and received my thought waves as I was thinking intently about my problems. Isn't this the way you recognized me?"

John Marshall nodded.

"It seems to have become dangerous to think at all; thoughts are no longer free," said Rhodan regretfully. "Since when can you read minds?"

"Ever since I was a child, though only at an unconscious level. Just a week ago I realized that I have telepathic powers. But I don't know why."

"When were you born?"

"Not too long after the Second World War. Why?"

Various possibilities crossed Rhodan's mind, combinations whizzed by, relays clicked, and then he knew the solution. "Atomic radiation, of course. Hiroshima, H bomb testing, fallout! There must be many more of you mutants running around in the world by now."

"Mutants?"

"Change of the genetic heritage. The radiation influenced

the structure of your brain when you were conceived." In the tiny pause that Perry Rhodan let intervene, another mighty vision of the future rose in front of his eye. Mutants! An entirely new perspective opened up before him. If he could find all these mutants, at least the most capable among them, and engage them for his cause, then he could create an unbeatable troop. Perhaps he would need such a troop at some future date. . . .

He stopped his thought, for he noticed the expression of amazement on Marshall's face. Perry Rhodan had almost forgotten that the other man was capable of reading his thoughts. Automatically he screened off his thoughts behind a barrier that would not let his thoughtwaves pass. This was one of the new abilities he had acquired during his hypnotraining with the indoctrinator.

"Why did you begin to talk to me?"

John Marshall smiled uncertainly. "I had intended to make money with my talents," he admitted frankly. "Since yesterday I have been negotiating with various institutions. They offered me huge sums of money. But I believe there are more important tasks for me. You just indicated this possibility in your thoughts."

Perry Rhodan breathed a sigh of relief. "You mean to say you would be willing to work for me?"

"Yes, indeed."

"But I am not in a position so far to pay you for your services."

"There are things that are more valuable than any amount of money—for instance, ideals."

"Ideals? What do you mean by that?"

"Isn't that the reason you are fighting against the whole world? It is not power alone that motivates you!"

"Power plays some role, too, I confess. But even power can help to make ideals come true."

"That's right! I am therefore ready and willing if you want me."

Perry took a closer look at the man. He liked him, quite apart from his special gifts. He held out his hand toward him. John Marshall took the profferred hand and shook it sincerely and firmly. Suddenly he looked beyond Rhodan.

His eyes narrowed behind his sunglasses. A strained expression replaced the look of joy on his face.

He whispered, "They are after you, Rhodan. That car across the street is an unmarked police car. It's just parking now behind your taxicab. Two men are getting out of it now—don't turn around! They are talking to the cabbie. They are coming here, toward our table. What do you suggest?"

Once again Rhodan's brain was working feverishly. One of the industrial managers must have given him away. Not intentionally, in all likelihood. Those guys from the International Intelligence Agency were not stupid at all. Once they picked up a scent, they did not let go of it until they tracked down their prey.

Rhodan was all ready when the two inconspicuously dressed gentlemen came to his table. He nodded imperceptibly to John, placed a five dollar bill under his plate, then got up. "We'll meet at the airport, then. In one hour. Wait for me there. They won't bother you."

John gave a slight nod. He got up and walked over to the next table as if the whole thing did not concern him in the least.

The two secret service agents hesitated for a fraction of a precious second before they approached Rhodan resolutely. One of them put his hand in his pocket; the other stepped up from behind and put his hand on Rhodan's shoulder.

"Perry Rhodan, in the name of all mankind—"

Rhodan turned around. His gray eyes pierced those of the agent. "What do you want?"

"You are Perry Rhodan."

"I am Foster Douglas, if you don't mind. Don't bother me!"

The agent hesitated. He had become unsure of himself. His colleague was unmoved. He withdrew his hand from his pocket. In it was a heavy gun.

"Don't make a wrong move now, Rhodan. Leave your hands just where they are. Come along with us!"

Perry Rhodan looked him straight in the eye. "I am Foster Douglas. Stop annoying me!" Several of the guests in the restaurant had turned to watch the scene. In the meantime John Marshall was walking leisurely toward the taxi stand near the next corner.

The second agent let his weapon hand drop. He was undecided what to do. Something deep inside him told him that he had made a mistake, that this man was not Perry Rhodan at all. And yet the old previous command was still working in him.

"You will not interfere now when I leave this place," said Rhodan, looking sharply at the two men. "You did not find Perry Rhodan. Inform your superiors accordingly. Is that clear?"

One of the men nodded, but the other was hesitant.

Rhodan turned around and walked off. He was ill at ease, for he could not protect himself from a bullet fired into his back. He wanted to switch on the energy screen only in case of the greatest emergency. And to fly off with his gravity neutralizer was impossible in broad daylight. They would send light airplanes after him at once.

The two agents were still standing there undecided when Rhodan stepped into his waiting taxi. Close behind it the police car was waiting. The driver held a microphone in his hand. He kept speaking into the mike. Obviously he could not figure out his colleagues' strange behavior.

"To the airport!" ordered Rhodan.

The taxi started moving and soon picked up speed.

The two agents seemed to rally from their shock. It was as if they were awakening from a bad dream. The table in front of them was unoccupied. Perry Rhodan had disappeared. Their bird had flown the coop. The diners in the restaurant were staring at them. The police car was waiting for them outside, but Rhodan's taxicab was no longer where it had been. It had disappeared too.

"What a dirty trick!" snorted the man with the gun, and ran out to their car, where he barked at the driver, "What's the matter with you? Why did you let him get away, you idiot?"

The driver put his microphone down. "Don't snap your thermostat, buddy. What are you blaming me for? It was you who let him get away. Wasn't that Rhodan?"

The other agent had joined them in the meantime. The

pressure in his brain had eased. His mind was functioning normally again.

"Hypnosis! We've fallen for that Rhodan's tricks. Which way did he go?"

The driver pointed down to the next corner to the right. "Over that way. Toward the airport."

"Let's get after him! Notify headquarters."

The police car tore around the corner at breakneck speed.

In the meantime John Marshall had found a taxi. Almost simultaneously with the police car he got onto the freeway. He leaned back in his seat, trying to catch the brainwaves of the excited agents. But he could not separate the confusion of the various "senders" in the police car. He could do nothing but urge his taxi driver not to lose sight of the big black car with the two agents and their driver.

The traffic observer in the helicopter hovering above the freeway observed three cars streaking along, weaving in and out of traffic. But the first car kept a constant distance, well ahead of the two others which closely followed each other. Although the freeway traffic was fairly heavy, the first car took but a few minutes to reach the parking lot near Global Airlines. Quickly Perry Rhodan paid the cab driver and ran toward the entrance. Soon he had disappeared among the crowd of arriving and departing travelers.

From somewhere came the sound of whining sirens. Policemen appeared suddenly at all the entrance and exit doors of the building. They were joined by men in civilian clothing. Their hands were in their baggy, bulging trouser pockets. The passengers in the air terminal became restless.

A loudspeaker blared above the busy din, "Keep calm, everybody! Police had to surround the building. This is an emergency measure. Just stay wherever you are. Don't move around!"

Rhodan knew that this was a civilian airport, but he had found out earlier in the day that at the end of one of the farther runways a fighter bomber of the IIA was was waiting, ready to depart at a moment's notice. The crew consisted of the pilot and three other men.

Rhodan was standing in the midst of a group of noisily arguing businessmen. They were furious at the prospect of missing their planes. About fifty yards from there John Marshall tried to push toward Rhodan in an inconspicuous manner. Both the agents from the restaurant were going from group to group, searching for their man.

Rhodan made a decision. He pushed down on a button at the belt of his Arkonide suit. At once the lightwave deflector began to work, and Rhodan became invisible.

Cautiously, trying to avoid bumping into anybody Rhodan moved toward John Marshall. The former bank employee was startled when he felt a disembodied touch from nowhere. Then Rhodan's thoughtwaves penetrated his brain.

Stop here Marshall, don't move on! I am invisible for the time being. They can't find me now. As soon as they don't see me any more they'll give up their search. They can't interrupt the traffic here in the airport any length of time.

Marshall nodded his assent. They waited.

"At the end of the farthest runway over there a fighter bomber of the IIA is waiting. We'll try to reach it. You *will* come with me, won't you, John?"

Marshall nodded.

"Good. We can't wait here forever. Start walking slowly toward that barrier over there. As soon as I become visible again, keep very close to me. I'll place an invisible energy screen around us both. That will afford complete protection. Then we'll walk toward the fighter bomber. Do you understand me?"

Once again Marshall nodded. Slowly he began to walk. The other passengers started moving too. They were fed up with the whole delay. They simply began to walk in all directions. Nobody could prevent them.

Marshall pulled out his passport for the employee at the barrier, who let him pass. Rhodan followed him closely, still invisible to the human eye. Then both men walked out onto the airfield. Several planes stood with motors running, ready to depart. Airport personnel and the police checked the papers of the passengers who were enplanning.

You keep on moving, Rhodan thought beamed.

Marshall walked past the first craft. All the way over to the left he had perceived the waiting fighter bomber.

Two men of the crew were lying stretched out under one of the wings, taking it easy in the shade. The pilot seemed to be checking out something at the landing gear. A fourth man was sitting inside the cabin, busy receiving instructions via radio.

Marshall walked calmly toward the bomber. The pilot interrupted what he was doing and looked with interest at John.

"Watch out! I am now going to materialize again. I'll become visible."

The pilot and the men resting in the shade under the wing opened their eyes wide in utter surprise when Rhodan's figure suddenly became visible next to Marshall. They did realize, though, what had happened for the simple reason that they had been waiting on standby because of Perry Rhodan. Who else but Rhodan was capable of becoming invisible at will?

The radio officer appeared in the door of the airplane.

"You will start right away!" commanded Perry Rhodan, looking forcefully at the pilot. "You will take us along with you. How much fuel do you have? Enough to fly nonstop across the Pacific?"

The pilot had somehow recovered from his initial shock; he smiled feebly. The radio officer had disappeared into the cabin in the meantime and now he returned with a pistol in his hand.

He aimed at Perry Rhodan. "Who are you?"

"It's Rhodan," replied the pilot. "Put that gun away. It wouldn't do you much good anyhow. After all, what harm would a bullet do to a man who can render himself invisible if he wants to? He is capable of anything! Isn't that so, Mr. Rhodan?"

Perry Rhodan confirmed the man's suspicion with a curt nod. "You haven't answered my question yet."

"You mean the fuel? We have enough to fly you halfway around the globe. Just get on. But hurry up—my colleagues over there are wondering what's wrong. They will be here any moment now."

"He is sincere," Marshall whispered to Rhodan. "He is on your side. Odd, isn't it?"

"How about the others?"

"They don't know what to do."

Rhodan turned to the pilot. "Why do you want to help me?"

"You are forcing me to help you. I just feel I must do whatever you ask me to. Hey, Jim! Hey, Hal! Get a move on. All aboard! Let's hurry. You too, Mr. Rhodan. Otherwise those guys will get here before we can take off."

Rhodan remained on the alert. Even after the machine was in the air, he remained suspicious. After all, these men were working for the IIA. But so did Captain Klein. And the bomber crew was coming to his assistance now, acting on a voluntary basis rather than under his hypnotic influence. They had gone over to his side, ignoring their original instructions from their superiors.

As the bomber raced westward, out toward the vast stretches of the Pacific Ocean, Rhodan felt something akin to gratitude. He was no longer alone; on the contrary, he had friends among the nations of the world, many friends. And suddenly he was impressed with the certainty that mankind *was* worthy of reigning over the galactic empire at some future date as partners of the Arkonides.

Captain Klein was in a bad mood.

He stood on a hill and looked toward the south. The huge sphere of the Arkonide spaceship stood out clearly against the bright horizon. The *Stardust I*, however, looked like a dark dot, tiny and unimpressive. At regular intervals mighty detonations could be heard, exploding against the invisible wall of energy that surrounded the *Stardust I* base.

Deep below the spot where Klein was standing the ground was vibrating, but he could not feel it. Gigantic drills were biting into the earth and excavating a shaft with frightening speed. Special commando troops were working day and night. Down below in the valley a small hill was building up from the dug out rock and dirt. The underground dynamite explosions were muffled by an intensified barrage aboveground against the energy dome.

There was no possibility at all of warning Rhodan. Numerous secret service agents were entrenched in outposts, waiting and keeping a close watch. The enemy's base had been completely isolated. Nobody could come anywhere near it without being noticed instantly. Way down deep, the shaft had already crossed the line that would have been the continuation of the energy wall if it had extended its effectiveness below ground. This meant, therefore, that they had penetrated into the fortress. All that was still needed was to change the direction of the underground tunnel. Just straight up. Then they would be inside the energy bell.

But the digging did not yet turn upward. The special machines continued boring their path southward and were approaching the point that, according to exact calculations, lay directly underneath the two spaceships. Another two days. Then the excavation of the tunnel would be completed. The hydrogen bomb was already on its way to the Gobi Desert.

Klein heard steps approaching from behind. It was Kosnow.

The Russian's face showed concern. "Rhodan is not inside the base," he said very softly, as if he were afraid someone might overhear their conversation. "Somebody recognized him in Los Angeles while he was negotiating for some machinery. According to the reports I have heard, he is supposed to have escaped in time in a fighter bomber of the IIA."

"Of all things," grinned Klein with amusement. "Then he will most likely turn up here very soon. There will be some fireworks!"

"I don't care, as long as we can warn him in time. He must know what is going on here in the meantime, what they are planning against him. In another two days they will change the direction of the underground shaft, and it will be bored straight up. There will be a tremendous increase in the bombardment against the energy wall, to drown out the noise from the underground vibrations. At a depth of approximately 150 feet underneath the spacecraft they'll detonate the H bomb. There won't be much left of Rhodan and his friends."

"There must be a way," Klein reassured him. "Even if it means that I have to get inside the dome myself to warn Perry Rhodan."

"It is absolutely impossible to get through the cordon

around the base. You know that they are suspicious of us. They don't trust us at all. And Mercant for sure knows that we deliberately did not carry out our mission to destroy Rhodan and the rest of his group."

"But Mercant doesn't do anything about it. I could almost believe that deep inside he is on Rhodan's side and therefore also on ours. But I can't understand, then, why he permits this attack! I am totally confused."

"He is forced to let them continue with their preparations to wipe out the so-called enemy of all mankind. He cannot yet openly show his true colors. He is just as convinced as we are that Rhodan did the right thing when he refused to surrender the power potential of the Arkonides into the hands of one government alone. But Mercant can't admit this yet. Perhaps someday soon he will be able to tell the truth about his own convictions."

"But what if Rhodan should be annihilated in the meantime?"

"It will never happen, even if I have to sacrifice my own life to prevent it. But the explosion of the bomb is still a long way off."

"And the tunnel has not yet been completed," confirmed Klein.

With a last glance at the distant spaceships, they turned north and walked down to the valley. Below they could see the Caterpillar tractors transporting the rocks and dirt that had been brought out from the underground shaft on a conveyor belt system. Everywhere there were groups of technicians standing around. Colonel Cretcher was talking with Lieutenant General Tai-tiang.

A man came running across the plain that had been crisscrossed by the innumerable tracks of vehicles and earth digging machinery. The man ran up to the general, saluted and handed him a message. Tai read it, then passed it on to Colonel Cretcher. Without waiting for a reply the general turned and walked briskly over to the next dugout. He disappeared quickly from view. Cretcher remained undecided for a moment, but then he, too, ran toward the trench and soon disappeared under the ground, running toward the entrance of the tunnel.

Kosnow frowned. He was puzzled by their odd behavior. "What was that all about?"

"Let's hurry and run after the messenger. If we can overtake him maybe we'll find out what's happened," suggested Klein. But before they had a chance to catch the man, the alarm sirens began to sound.

"There goes the alarm! Something must be wrong."

Just as the messenger was about to disappear into his tent, Klein got hold of his sleeve. "What's going on here?"

"Rhodan!" shouted the man, a Chinese soldier. His English was broken. "He steal airplane . . ."

"That isn't the reason for the alarm. We have all known this since yesterday."

"He come here, this Rhodan. In five minutes, he be here."

Klein exchanged a glance with Kosnow. That was what all the commotion was about!

They ran off toward the entrance of the shaft, leaving a most bewildered soldier behind. If the news was correct, then all hell would break loose here within the next five minutes. They would try to prevent Rhodan from reaching the safety of his base at all costs. Or else . . .

Another possible solution flashed through Klein's mind. Maybe they did not intend at all to prevent Rhodan from passing through the protective energy screen that surrounds his base. There were plenty of reasons why they shouldn't. But would General Tai be aware of these reasons?

"Let's go, Kosnow! To the general! I have just had a brainstorm!"

Tai looked up surprised as the two entered his command post. He had just established communication with his gun emplacements and was about to issue his orders to them.

"What's the matter? How dare you . . . ?"

"Withdraw your orders at once!" requested Klein firmly.

"What do you know about it?"

"Rhodan has stolen an airplane and will be trying to land it just outside the energy dome. You want to prevent him from doing so. Do you realize what might be the consequences if he notices your plan against him? That same moment he will turn around and simply go into hiding somewhere. What good would it do us to detonate a bomb under the base if Rhodan is not inside it and wouldn't be destroyed with it?"

Lieutenant General Tai could react very fast, if necessary. He contemplated Klein for a brief second with appreciation; then he nodded. "Not bad, this suggestion. You're right. I will let Rhodan land without any interference and enter his base. He won't get away. He will be caught right in the trap. The big bomb is already on its way. We completed our tunnel construction sooner than planned, I have just learned from Colonel Cretcher. I will inform the pursuing fighter planes to that effect immediately."

With these words he took off toward the communications tent.

Klein and Kosnow, however, climbed up on the hill again so they could witness the imminent landing of Rhodan's plane.

They did not have long to wait. A tiny dot appeared on the horizon. It rapidly grew larger and could be recognized as a fighter bomber of the latest design. A few smaller aircraft flew beside it, trying to push it toward the ground. But they did not shoot at the fugitive bomber, to avoid endangering the lives of its crew members.

Rhodan was standing beside the pilot. "You have done a splendid job, very brave indeed. I am very grateful for your help. Perhaps I can return the favor someday. Please land now exactly at the spot that I will point out to you. Nothing will happen to you or your crew—you can swear that I forced you to bring me here. Soon Mr. Marshall and I will be leaving you. It will be just a few steps from the landing site to the energy wall."

"How will we manage to get through that wall?" asked John Marshall from inside the cabin.

"I have some special equipment to neutralize the screen at any spot I choose. In a few seconds we will make it to safety. What matters now is to land before the fighter planes know *where* we touch down."

The bomber prepared for landing.

"I wonder why we hadn't been met by a welcoming committee of flak fire," said the pilot.

The radio operator, with earphones clamped on his head,

gave the explanation. "They withdrew their order to open fire on us. No reason was given for it. Might be that our lives are too precious. They probably want to interrogate us, and dead people don't talk."

The wheels touched the ground. The plane seemed to sway, then advanced by a few irregular giant hops and ran into a huge boulder. Rhodan estimated it was about a hundred yards to the energy wall.

The impact threw the pilot against the instrument panel. His features contorted painfully as he instinctively shut off the fuel. The radio operator climbed out from underneath his shattered sets. The two other members of the crew were already opening the exit hatch.

"Many thanks again! And lots of luck to you!" called Perry Rhodan as he pulled John Marshall out onto the ground with him. "We must run as fast as we can; otherwise, they might get us before we reach the wall. Stay very close to me now. I'm switching on my special portable screen."

They began racing toward the spaceships that stood about three miles from them in the center of the base. Rhodan held tight to Marshall's hand and pushed a button on his belt. Nothing seemed to have changed around them, except for a sudden cessation of wind. Their small energy bell protected and isolated them completely from the outside world.

One of the fighter planes banked in a wide loop and approached the two men, flying very low. Guns blazed from underneath the wings. Four parallel lines of bullets tore into the earth, coming steadily closer to Rhodan and Marshall. John screamed out loud.

Then the firing ceased.

"Don't be afraid, Marshall. They'd need *much* heavier guns to pierce this protective shell around us."

The fighter plane banked to the right, seemed to gain altitude and all of a sudden smashed against an invisible obstacle in midair. The force of the impact was so tremendous that the craft was squashed flat as a pancake. Then it rolled downhill on an invisible slope and finally hit the ground. Flames out of the wrecked airplane, and in a moment the ammunition it had carried exploded and entirely destroyed the fighter.

"Watch out, here comes the energy wall just a few feet ahead of us. Look out now—I'm applying the neutralizer equipment. Don't worry, the other fighter planes are too late already. When we're finally safe inside, you can move about freely."

Perry Rhodan released his grip on Marshall's hand. He looked back over his shoulder and saw the other fighter planes climb quickly out of danger. They soon disappeared in the south. Next to the fighter bomber they had left a little while ago, the four members of the crew stood and waved farewell. Then the crew of the stolen plane turned and marched off toward the far distant lines of the encircling troops. They knew that they would have to face some rather unpleasant hours being interrogated.

"Come on, Marshall. Over there is the *Stardust* waiting for us. And may I welcome you most cordially to my domain!"

"Thank you very much," replied John Marshall. As Rhodan kept a straight course toward the two spaceships waiting in the middle of the desert, Marshall walked by his side.

They almost tripped over a man who suddenly appeared out of nothingness in front of them. He regarded them with frightened eyes.

Rhodan stopped abruptly.

The flat expanse of sand was devoid of any protective cover. . . .

CHAPTER SIX

THE TORPEDO SHAPED machine was eating into the rock with enormous speed. The finely ground stone slid automatically onto the conveyor belt and was carried to the surface. Many cables supplied the needed current for machines and illumination. The air conditioning system worked most efficiently.

Colonel Cretcher was standing next to Klein and Li. His face bore an expression of supreme satisfaction.

"What a splendid idea you had, Klein, to convince Tai not to open fire on Rhodan. I won't forget to mention this to Mr. Mercant, rest assured."

"He will be pleased about it, I am sure," ventured Klein, smiling inwardly at the hidden double meaning of his remark.

Lieutenant Li pointed to the earth excavator. "How much longer?"

"Tomorrow night. The vertical shaft toward the surface is going to be just wide enough to let the H bomb pass through. The day after tomorrow there will be no more Perry Rhodan—and no Arkonides, either."

"The whole world will be able to breathe easier," muttered Klein.

Cretcher glanced at him briefly. "Possibly," he said, then turned his attention once again to the gigantic earth digging machines.

Klein and Li walked back along the tunnel toward the exit. The corridor was about six feet high and well lit. The walls were smooth. The conveyor belt was glided noiselessly on their left on its uninterrupted way to the exit. There was no one in sight.

"We must warn Rhodan," whispered Klein desperately. "Tomorrow will be too late. I can't imagine how he could foil this H bomb detonation, even if he found out about it right now."

"Don't talk so loud," breathed Li. "Sound carries too well here under these conditions. But you are right. I can't figure out any way out either. I feel as if I were about to betray Perry Rhodan. What will happen if their dastardly plan succeeds and Rhodan and his friends are all killed? I can tell you—the day after their death we will witness the renewal of the Cold War and, with it, our constant fear of the inevitable atomic destruction of the world. I don't know how much longer this can go on."

Klein stopped suddenly. "Tonight I will try to pass through the lines of the secret front trenches."

The Chinese shook his head. "Even if you should manage to get through the front lines, what would you have accomplished? Do you really believe that Rhodan can keep constant watch along the whole extent of his borders? He won't even notice you standing and waiting to talk to him at the edge of his domain. No, it won't work. We must draw his attention to us in some other way—but if I only knew how!"

"Shush, somebody is coming," whispered Klein. They had heard the steps in time. A man walked toward them, coming from the entrance of the shaft. As they walked past each other, they recognized him as Tako Kakuta, one of the Japanese technicians. His gentle eyes searched theirs; his narrow chest was heaving.

"Hi, Tako. We've almost made it, haven't we?"

"Yes, sir, I believe so," replied the Japanese cautiously. "Is Colonel Cretcher up there ahead?"

"Yes, he is near the excavating machine," confirmed Klein, and continued on his way. Li tried to keep up with him. They had a long way to go before they would arrive at the exit, but they sat down on the conveyor belt as soon as they got too tired. This way they made much better time, too.

They could already see the brightly shining opening of the shaft far ahead of them, when suddenly they became aware of a shadow silhouetted against the daylight. They made it out to be the figure of a man walking toward the exit. Riding on the speedy conveyor belt, they managed to overtake the stranger as he walked past a very bright arc light. Klein's jaw dropped in amazement when he recognized the man. In utter disbelief he turned around, then jumped off the belt onto the ground. Li did not react as swiftly as Klein and was carried on by the belt. Klein waited until the walking man came close.

It was Tako Kakuta.

The passage was not wide. The Japanese had gone all the way back to talk with Colonel Cretcher about twenty minutes ago. In the meantime Klein and Li had hurried toward the tunnel entrance. And now they had overtaken the Japanese, arriving close to the exit almost simultaneously with them.

That was absolutely impossible!

Klein's thoughts raced, his brain trying feverishly to find a logical explanation for this seemingly impossible feat.

Tako kept smiling, his feelings hidden under an impenetrable mask. He spoke almost humbly. "We must somehow have missed each other, Mr. Klein, on our way back."

Klein could not accept this and slowly shook his head. "How did you get here so quickly, Tako? You will have to tell me. I am one of the patrolling security officers here in the tunnel. You can't possibly have passed by us. On the contrary, you should just now have arrived at Colonel Cretcher's position. Tell me—how did you manage to get here?"

The Japanese kept smiling. "I have overtaken you, sir."

"That's a lie, and you know it! We would have noticed you coming by. Let's hear the truth now!"

For the first time something like fear appeared in the eyes of the thin Japanese. "You would not believe the truth, even if I told it to you," he said earnestly. "Please forget the incident. I have nothing more to add."

"But I have a lot to tell you," countered Klein, and seized the arm of the Japanese. "Come along—"

His hand suddenly clasped emptiness. The Japanese

had vanished. He had dissolved into nothingness or perhaps become invisible. Klein was standing dumbfounded when Li reached him.

"What's the matter, Klein? Where is Tako?"

Klein seemed to wake up from a bad dream. "If only I knew! The same way he made his appearance here, the same way he also disappeared again. Either I am suffering from hallucinations or . . ."

"Or?"

"Or he knows how to render himself invisible to our eyes, Li! But such things don't exist! Nobody can make himself invisible!"

Li stared at the smooth wall of rock. "There is some other solution to this phenomenon. I have heard of similar cases where people suddenly vanished and then reappeared at some other place."

"Come on now, Li, we are living in the twentieth century!"

"That's exactly it. It could only have happened in our century. Haven't you ever heard of mutations? Activation of parts of the brain that had been dormant so far? People that have been affected this way have discovered in themselves some talents that had never been encountered before. Tako might be one of those people. I would guess that his speciality is teleportation."

"And what is that supposed to be?"

"It means that Tako is capable of transporting himself to some other place simply by the power of his own will. This sounds like a fairy tale, I know, but it can be accomplished under the right circumstances."

"Under which circumstances?"

Li became very serious.

"Nuclear radiation. Fallout from atom bombs. The children that were born after the detonation of the atom bombs over Hiroshima and Nagasaki, the children that were conceived and that grew up in the age of constant H bomb testing, these children have now reached adulthood. Their incipient faculties have developed with increasing maturity. There are mutants now living all over the world. I don't dare imagine what mankind will be like in another fifty years."

Klein had grown pale. "You're crazy! There might be some occasional exceptions, nothing more than that. Provided what you say is really the case."

"Not exceptions, Mr. Klein. They will be the norm. And man the way he is today will become the exception at some time in the future. But let's hurry now. We must find Tako and talk to him. We must know if he really is a mutant."

And while they were searching for him, Klein found the answer he had been looking for.

If they could bring Tako over to their side, they would have the way out they had been seeking. Tako could warn Rhodan of the impending catastrophe.

"Of course I could have escaped," said Tako humbly. "But this would not have helped me very much. You would have kept on hunting for me, and finally you would have caught up with me. This is why I followed you here. And now you can ask me all you want."

The door was locked. They were alone in the room. Li stood watch outside. Nobody could surprise them here.

"Are you a natural mutant?"

"My parents survived the catastrophe in Hiroshima. Sometime later I was born. My mother died still young as a result of the radiation she had received. My father was crippled. I was the only one to grow up healthy among my brothers and sisters. About a year ago I discovered the special ability that you witnessed today in the tunnel. I've tried to develop this ability on my own, but I am convinced that I have not yet reached my full potential. Well, what are you going to do with me now, Mr. Klein?"

"You don't have to be afraid, Tako. How far can you travel this way?"

"Approximately one-third of a mile, not more than that. If I want to travel longer distances I must do it in several steps."

"Only a third of a mile," Klein could not hide his disappointment. "That is not too much. What happens if you materialize in the middle of some solid object and not in the air?"

Tako smiled. "That is impossible. Then the next jump

follows automatically. I cannot exert too much influence on this process, but I can regulate the first step quite accurately, so that I run hardly any risk in my travels."

Klein breathed deeply before he ventured his next question. "I would like to ask you something, Tako. Do you hate Perry Rhodan, the man we are supposed to annihilate with the H bomb?"

Tako retained his inscrutable smile. "You are an officer and part of the defense system. It is your duty to watch over the security of this special enterprise. If I did not hate Rhodan I could still not tell you so. Don't you agree?"

"You are right. But I did not intend this to be a catch question. I wanted to find out what you really think about Rhodan. Now I am risking my neck when I tell you what my opinion is in this respect. But you see, I have confidence in you. Tako, this enterprise I have to supervise must not succeed! Rhodan must not be killed! Do you understand me, Tako? If Rhodan should be wiped out tomorrow by this H bomb, then similar mushroom clouds will rise over all the continents in the near future. Life on Earth will come to an end. Only the Third Power is capable of preventing this last of all wars. It is difficult to comprehend but it is the logical conclusion from the events that have led up to this day.

"Well, now you are informed of my innermost thoughts —may I know now what you think?"

Tako's facial expression remained unchanged. "Perry Rhodan has far more friends today than he has hoped for. These friends must remain underground, though, for even the mighty are fearful in the face of the still more powerful. You see, Mr. Klein, your fear is unfounded. But what can an individual do but execute the orders of his society? Is it possible for the isolated person to revolt against those in power?"

"Not the individual, but it is possible for the many isolated people banded together. United, they produce a factor of power that no one can comprehend. And in regard to your question—we *can* avoid the catastrophe, for now we have you, Tako, on our side."

"How can I be of help?"

"You will approach Rhodan and warn him of the danger. Nobody else can penetrate into their fortress, but I assume that the energy barrier can't hold you back. Am I right?"

"Yes, indeed. I can get through the energy wall unimpeded."

Klein was startled. "How can you be so sure of that?"

"I can get through it. But why should I still hold back with anything? We no longer have anything to conceal from each other. You wanted to send me to Rhodan to warn him, isn't that so?"

Klein nodded.

"Well, I had the same idea you did. I already have warned him, Mr. Klein. I would strongly suggest that you not enter the tunnel after this midnight. That is the deadline Rhodan set when he learned of the planned nuclear attack."

Klein stared at Tako, completely baffled. Then he added with a tone of hope, "You were right, Tako, when you said that Rhodan already has more friends than he dares to hope for."

CHAPTER SEVEN

THE MAN WAS a Japanese, Rhodan noticed at once. The man bowed deeply and humbly, his face smiling like that of a child.

"Please don't be frightened, Mr. Rhodan. But I have come here to warn you of a great danger."

"How did you get through the energy barrier?" Rhodan asked, recovering from his initial shock. Probably he had only overlooked this young man here in the bright desert sun. "I noticed you so suddenly. You seemed to appear out of nowhere."

"I am capable of teleportation."

John Marshall whispered in Rhodan's ear, "He is a mutant. Just like I am. He can transport himself from one place to the other without any interval of time. He has come from down below there."

"From down below?"

"Yes," replied Tako. "I came from down there. From an underground shaft running below your domain. But . . ." He hesitated and turned to Marshall. "How do you know this?"

Marshall stepped closer. "I am a mutant, the same as you are, Tako Kakuta. That's your name, isn't it? You are capable of teleportation, and I can read minds." He stretched out his hand in a friendly gesture. "We are colleagues in a certain way. You have come to help Perry Rhodan."

Tako shook the hand held out to him. "Yes, that is why I have come here. He has prevented the atomic war. All mankind should be grateful to him for having saved their lives. But human beings are unfortunately rather stupid."

Rhodan had completely regained his composure. He had

found the second mutant. What he had only presumed so far had now been confirmed. This would provide a real basis for his secret plan to gather around him a small group of mutants who would be able to aid and protect him with the help of their superior abilities.

"What is the great danger you came here to warn me of, Tako?"

"A special detachment is busy constructing a tunnel that will end 150 feet directly below your spacecraft. Tomorrow they will explode there a hydrogen bomb. I doubt that anything will remain of your installations unless you take some fast counteraction."

"They'll detonate a bomb directly underneath our base?" Rhodan grew pale for a fraction of a second. Then his brain began to work with lightning speed and comprehended immediately the proper defensive measures.

"Thank you, Tako. I think that it is not advisable for you to return to the outside. You may stay here with me if you wish."

"Gladly. But only later," the Japanese said modestly. "I assume that you are going to defend yourself against the nuclear attack. It is my duty to prevent loss of life among my comrades. May I ask you what you plan to do?"

"I haven't decided yet in detail," admitted Rhodan. "In any case, I won't start with any counteroffensive before tonight. Will that information be enough for you?"

"I will take care that nobody will remain inside the shaft tonight."

Rhodan put his hand on Tako's shoulder and spoke with appreciation. "You display a very humane attitude, my friend."

"Anyone would do that in my position, that is, anyone whose parents lived through an atomic attack. We will meet again very soon. Till then, Perry Rhodan."

The Japanese vanished right in front of their eyes. No trace remained of his presence. In the distance the two men could make out the glittering shapes of the spaceships. Someone was walking toward them, still far away.

"What was he really thinking?" inquired Rhodan.

John Marshall replied with emphasis, "His thoughts and his words were exactly the same."

"Good. Then he spoke the truth. Let's go—here comes Reg."

"Reg?"

"My friend Reginald Bell, second pilot and technician of the moonship *Stardust*."

They met up with Reginald Bell about half a mile from the center of the base.

"Glad you're back with us again, Perry. And you brought along a visitor. Introduce us, will you?"

But before Rhodan had a chance, John Marshall remarked dryly, "To begin with, I never use any hair oil, my dear Mr. Bell. That's the way my hair is naturally, smooth and slick. Secondly, you are no great beauty either. And finally, it's none of your infernal business *how* I managed to get into Perry Rhodan's good graces."

Bell's red hair stood up like a brush, and his lower jaw dropped. With a helpless expression he stared first at Marshall and then at Perry Rhodan.

"For crying out loud!" he said. "That guy knows exactly what I was thinking to myself!"

"Yes, Reg. He can read minds," said Rhodan, who could hardly refrain from laughing. "If I were you I would be more careful in the future; or if you want to have the luxury of your own private thoughts, why don't you surround your brainwave field with a protective barrier, the way we learned during our hypno training? By the way, allow me to introduce you to the first known telepath to develop in a slowly awakening mankind."

"Glad to know you," mumbled Reg, who was still struck with awe at this frightening display of invasion of privacy.

"My pleasure," replied John. "At least you will keep your thoughts nicely fenced in from now on and not embarrass any strangers with your critical silent remarks."

Rhodan interjected abruptly, "Is everything okay here?"

"Everything is fine, boss."

"Good. Let's go. I must have a talk with Khrest at once. It's urgent. They are getting ready to attack us. They plan to blow us all up. Nice, friendly people around here, don't you agree?"

"Real nice of them. But how do they propose to do that?"

"They built a shaft from their lines to a point immediately below our position here."

"How did you find this out?"

"I can tell you that only later. There's not enough time now."

Khrest was waiting for them in front of the space sphere. Eric Manoli was at his side, and Dr. Haggard stood a few paces behind them. In the background Thora was busy supervising a few robots who were building some machinery.

"I am happy to see that you have returned safely," Khrest greeted his first and foremost ally on the planet Earth. "Was your mission successful?"

"Please, Khrest, will you call Thora immediately? We must act at once, otherwise, we shall be lost. The power blocs of the world are collaborating, and that makes them dangerous for us. They failed to penetrate the energy screen, but they have found another way to get at us. They drove a shaft to right underneath this spaceship. Tomorrow they will explode a hydrogen bomb down there."

"You brought a guest with you?" inquired Khrest, without even mentioning the threatening danger. "He is a telepath—I can feel it. That means that mankind has overcome another hurdle toward maturity. Welcome, Mr. Marshall. My brain has the same capacity for telepathy, but I don't make much use of it. What did you say, Perry? A shaft? A bomb? Thora will be pleased to hear that."

The irony was not lost on them. Thora's reaction to the news was full of hatred and disdain. "They'll never learn. The time has come to teach them a good lesson that they won't soon forget."

The five men sat together with Khrest and Thora in a comfortably furnished cabin of the space sphere. Dusk was falling outside in the desert.

"I strongly warn you against any rash decision." Khrest chided her. "All that is necessary here is to foil their aggressive and destructive plans."

"If I had my way I would exterminate the whole race," replied Thora fiercely.

"This would be not only most unwise but also most dangerous. You know we can't return to our home planet, Arkon, without help. And who knows whether another intelligent race can be found within a radius of 500 light-years."

These sobering words had their intended effect on Thora. She nodded her consent, though reluctantly. "I'll abide by the decision of the majority. What are we going to do?"

Rhodan bent forward. "Is there any chance of destroying this tunnel from where we are?"

"Yes. The direction finder has already indicated the position of the tunnel. I will apply the focal ray projector."

"What is that?"

"A special kind of energy. It emanates from the generator and the transformer in the form of harmless waves, and only when it arrives at its intended destination is it changed into a destructive type of energy. That means that from here I can send an energy ray through any matter without damaging it. But one mile from here, or even 150 feet below the ground, the desired destructive effect will take place. The direction finder indicates the exact location of the tunnel. I focus on this point with the focal ray projector. This will cause the whole shaft to liquefy into molten rock. Will that do, I hope?"

Rhodan smiled gently. "It will certainly do. A great deal can happen before they decide to attack us anew. I hardly believe that they will consider us their deadly enemies for very long. It seems that gradually they learn to look upon us in a different way, to realize that we can offer them a great many advantages. We already have many more sympathizers among mankind than we imagine."

"That would please me greatly," said Khrest with warmth.

Thora interrupted, "When is the action going to take place?"

Rhodan looked at his watch. "Ten hours from now, Thora. There won't be a living soul in the tunnel at that time."

She did not look at him. "All right. But rest assured, Rhodan, this will be the last time that I will be considerate of the feelings of anyone. The next attack will be answered by a total destruction of your race. It might be wise to inform your people accordingly."

She got up and walked haughtily out of the room without so much as turning around once.

John Marshall interrupted the silence and addressed Rhodan. "Strange . . . she is lying. She is thinking differently from the way she speaks."

A gray dawn was rising far to the east.

The others were fast asleep. Perry Rhodan and Reginald Bell sat and waited together in the command center of the *Stardust*. Again and again they glanced over at the clock on the wall. How slowly the hands were creeping ahead! Still four more minutes to go until 4 A.M.

Across the road they could see the lights burning in the space sphere. A slender shadow showed itself from time to time behind one of the windows. It was Thora, standing in front of the electronic complex that she had called the focal ray projector. Her hand might at any moment grasp one of the many levers.

"Will she keep her word?" whispered Bell.

"I am sure she will," Rhodan reassured him. Then he continued. "Our Japanese friend must have been able to evacuate the tunnel, otherwise, he would have let us know. He would have requested a further delay. And with the four extra hours we gave them . . . Reg, she is starting!"

A green light came from the space sphere. Its glow mingled eerily with the dawn's light.

Deep below the surface of the earth, the unleashed atomic forces melted the products of human technology to unrecognizable lumps of metal. The walls of solid rock turned to liquid streams that congealed in bizarre shapes. Layers of loose gravel slid down and evaporated with a hissing noise. Slowly the holocaust advanced toward the entrance of the shaft.

The soldier standing guard near the entrance first noticed a pleasant rise in the temperature of the chilly nocturnal air. Then vapors welled up from the tunnel and filled his nostrils and lungs with their acrid odor. Horrified, he sounded the alarm. A few seconds later the whole camp had come alive. Molten rock oozed out of the tunnel entrance and solidified in big chunks that effectively blocked the entrance. A huge, impenetrable plug had been placed in the steaming opening of the cave.

Klein turned away from the window. "That is the end

of that tunnel, Tako. You rendered a tremendous service to us and to all mankind when you warned Rhodan. Also when you made sure that nobody had remained in the shaft tonight."

"It was not easy to convince Colonel Cretcher that there was radioactivity inside the tunnel. Fortunately, I managed to hunt up a few ounces of uranium and place it inside the shaft."

Li and Kosnow got up and shook hands with the Japanese to thank him for his deed.

"You will say hello to Perry Rhodan from us?" Klein asked. "Tell him that he can always count on us. And don't forget to mention that we are impatiently waiting for the day when we can join him officially."

"I will give him your regards, don't worry," promised Tako. "There will be many opportunities for us to show him our loyalty. Goodbye for now. . . ."

A second later the three men were left alone.

And Tako materialized inside the command center of the *Stardust*.

Reg was standing with his back against the window, yawning loudly. "It's probably all over by now," he groaned. "I'm dead tired. I'm going to bed."

Suddenly a human figure appeared out of thin air about three feet in front of him. The man bowed slightly and said to Rhodan, "I have completed my mission, Mr. Rhodan. Now I am coming to offer my services to you."

Despite his swiftly reacting brain, Reg's surprise was stronger than his logical mind. Although Rhodan had told him that Tako was a teleporter, this sudden apparition from nowhere startled him. First somebody read his thoughts, and now this! He stood motionless and stared at the Japanese.

"Snap your trap, Reg, or you might swallow Tako!" Rhodan said. He turned to the Japanese. "I accept your offer, Tako. Your forces and Marshall's combined represent a tremendous force. I know that we will be successful."

"If I had not shared this belief I would not have joined you," declared the Japanese, pride shining in his eyes.

Reg finally closed his mouth. He half shut his eyes

and cautiously stretched out his hands. Then he placed them on Tako's shoulders. "He is for real!"

"Of course he is," smiled Rhodan. "Or did you think he was a ghost?"

"Can he do that trick any time and any place he wants to go?"

"Yes, indeed."

A sparkle appeared in Bell's eyes. "Even to the space sphere of the Arkonides?"

"And why not?"

Reg grinned hugely. "Tako, could you please check if Thora has already completed her counterattack against the enemy? It's okay, Perry, isn't it? There is nothing wrong with that?"

Perry Rhodan frowned slightly. "We would save ourselves a trip over there. What do you think, Tako—can you do that for us?"

The Japanese peered through the hatch toward the space sphere. There were still some lights burning here and there.

"All right." Before Reg could say a word, Tako had vanished.

A few seconds passed, and then Bell remarked, "I hope she gets a good scare, when suddenly somebody—"

But he himself was on the receiving end, for he was thoroughly frightened when Tako reappeared the same instant. An apologetic smile played around his lips.

"I am sorry but I could not talk to Thora. She was just getting ready to retire."

Now it was Rhodan's turn to smile in amusement. "And . . . ?"

"Yes, and . . . ?" Bell asked with a triumphant grin. "Did she get good and scared?"

"She did not even notice me. I materialized directly in back of her. She was just removing her garment."

"Her garment?" Reg opened his eyes wide in delight. A radiant expression covered his face, and he put both hands on Tako's shoulders. "We have become good friends, Tako, haven't we? And we will be closer friends still. Is that all right with you?"

"Of course," stammered the Japanese in consternation. "Why do you ask me that?"

Reg whispered in Tako's ear, "You must teach me teleportation—you simply *must*."

And he led a nonplussed Tako out of the command center to show him to his quarters.

Perry Rhodan watched them leave the room. He smiled in amusement. Then, before he retired, he looked once again out into the desert.

The desert stretched before him, empty and peaceful.

The starry sky of night began to change color. It became a deep red. A new day was beginning. What would it have in store for them?

Enterprise Stardust

PERILOUS DAWN . . .

Major Perry Rhodan, commander of the spaceship
STARDUST, found more than anyone had expected
might exist on the moon — for he became the first
man to make contact with another sentient race!

The Arkonides had come from a distant star, and
they possessed a knowledge of science and
philosophy that dwarfed mankind's knowledge.

But these enormously powerful alien beings
refused to cooperate with the people of Earth . . .
unless Perry Rhodan could pass the most difficult
test any human being had ever faced . . .

ENTERPRISE STARDUST is the first novel
in the Perry Rhodan series which sold
more than 70 million copies in
Europe and America.

Dwellers in the Mirage

Beneath the shimmering surface of a lake cradled in the desolate Alaskan mountains, the people of the Shadowed-Land waited for Dwayanu, the warrior hero who will bring back to the world th worship of Khalk'ru, the cruel, destructive octopus god whose appetites must be appeased by human sacrifice.

When Lief Langdon accidentally discovers the people beneath the valley floor, they welcome him a the reincarnation of Dwayanu. Slowly Langdon's personality is possessed by the pride and blood-lust of his warrior ancestor until he is driven by forces beyond his understanding or control to serve the evil power of Khalk'ru.

A classic of science fiction, DWELLERS IN THE MIRAGE weaves a powerful web of fantasy against a background of lost civilisations.

The Face in the Abyss

A remote valley hidden amid the towering peaks of the Andes and never before visited by civilised man is the scene of A. A. Merritt's classic novel of supernatural fantasy. The valley is inhabited by creatures long forgotten and races pledged to the resurrection of the glorious past.

Into this valley stumbles a young mining engineer, Nicholas Graydon. He defies the commands of the Snake-Mother's invisible but deadly servants and returns to the forbidden valley for the sake of Suarra, whom he loves. But Suarra can not be his until Graydon has persuaded the Snake-Mother to free the land of Yu-Atlanchi from Nimir, the Shadow of Evil. And the way to the Snake-Mother is beset with perils. Such as Lantlu, rider of dinosoaurs; the Lizard men. And, of course, the Dark Lord himself.

THOR HEYERDAHL
Sea Routes to Polynesia

WHO WERE THE POLYNESIANS?

When Thor Heyerdahl first suggested that the Polynesian Islands could have been colonised in prehistoric times by South American Indians who crossed the Pacific on wooden rafts, many of the experts remained sceptical. How, they asked, could the frail reed and balsa wood rafts of the South American Indians have spanned such enormous distances?

The *Kon-Tiki* expedition proved that it was possible: now, in *Sea Routes to Polynesia*, Thor Heyerdahl explores the theories behind his epic voyage, describes his subsequent discoveries and provides a fascinating insight into the islands, peoples and customs of the Pacific from the Malay peninsular to the coast of Ecuador, from the aborigines of the Galapagos to the statues of Rano-Raraku on Easter Island.